D1245729

What the critics are saying…

Four blue ribbons! "Hot! Steamy! Sexy! Explosive! These are the words to describe Lorie O'Clare's IN HER SOUL." *Romance Junkies*

"This book was a one sitting read with strong characters, a great plot, and hot sex." *M. Jeffers The Road To Romance*

"In Her Soul is a real page-turner, Trudy and Adam generate enough heat to light up the NYC skyline." *Joy Coffee Time Romance*

IN HER SOUL
LUNEWULF

Lorie O'Clare

IN HER SOUL
An Ellora's Cave Publication, March 2005

Ellora's Cave Publishing, Inc.
1337 Commerce Drive, Suite #13
Stow, Ohio 44224

ISBN #1419951688

IN HER SOUL Copyright © 2004 Lorie O'Clare
Other available formats: ISBN MS Reader (LIT), Adobe (PDF),
Rocketbook (RB), Mobipocket (PRC) & HTML

ALL RIGHTS RESERVED. This book may not be reproduced in
whole or in part without permission.

This book is a work of fiction and any resemblance to persons,
living or dead, or places, events or locales is purely coincidental.
They are productions of the authors' imagination and used
fictitiously.

Edited by: *Briana St. James*
Cover art by: *Syneca*

Warning:

The following material contains graphic sexual content meant for mature readers. *In Her Soul* has been rated *E-rotic* by a minimum of three independent reviewers.

Ellora's Cave Publishing offers three levels of Romantica™ reading entertainment: S (S-ensuous), E (E-rotic), and X (X-treme).

S-*ensuous* love scenes are explicit and leave nothing to the imagination.

E-*rotic* love scenes are explicit, leave nothing to the imagination, and are high in volume per the overall word count. In addition, some E-rated titles might contain fantasy material that some readers find objectionable, such as bondage, submission, same sex encounters, forced seductions, etc. E-rated titles are the most graphic titles we carry; it is common, for instance, for an author to use words such as "fucking", "cock", "pussy", etc., within their work of literature.

X-*treme* titles differ from E-rated titles only in plot premise and storyline execution. Unlike E-rated titles, stories designated with the letter X tend to contain controversial subject matter not for the faint of heart.

Also by Lorie O'Clare:

IN HER SOUL

LUNEWULF

Chapter One

The bouncer took her wrist, stamping a nondescript image on the back of her hand. Trudy Rousseau barely glanced at it, focusing instead on the people mingling beyond the entrance.

"Looking for someone?" The bouncer had beer on his breath.

"I'll find them." She brushed past him, determined to make the best of the night and have fun.

A young man who couldn't possibly be twenty-one gave her a toothy grin as he stepped in her path. Trudy avoided getting a rum and coke spilled on her. "Excuse me. I'm sorry," she said, dodging around the rather intoxicated human. She caught glimpses of the bar.

There were werewolves here. The earthy aroma couldn't be missed. But with so many people, the mixed odors filled the air, making it hard to distinguish direction of scent.

"Want to dance?" A young human, barely old enough to shave, moved in front of her.

A sultry beat pounded from the dance floor. People merged on to the tiled floor in the middle of the club. Sexual aromas lingered everywhere. Typical of a pick-up bar, a meat market.

"Ask me later." Trudy smiled at the young human, but then took advantage of the crowd to lose him, continuing her path toward the bar.

Lust and desire drifted around her, their rich, sweet aromas mixing with body sweat and alcohol. Humans fornicating. How blasé. The species had no clue how to let loose and really fuck.

Humans always hesitated. She craved a mate she could truly be herself with. Not forced into the submissive role like her previous mate had required. She wanted wild, aggressive sex, with a partner who wouldn't hold back.

Elsa's mate, Rick Bolton, had arranged for her to meet werewolves who used to belong to his pack. Excitement still tingled through her after winning the argument over her traveling alone.

"I traveled alone." Elsa had stood up for her. "And Trudy is the oldest in our den, and a widowed bitch. She'll do just fine."

Considering she'd never been out of British Columbia before, Trudy decided she was doing damned fine. And now, of all places, here she was at a nightclub in Fargo, North Dakota, surrounded by Americans. She'd heard the rumors about how American werewolves were less disciplined, more rough around the collar. She couldn't wait to get to know some of them.

"Give me another gin and orange juice." The lady next to Trudy held her empty glass up in the air, catching the bartender's attention.

Trudy squeezed in next to the woman. Strobe lights matched the beat of the music on the dance floor. The primal rhythm pounded through her, while flashing lights tampered with her vision. At the same time, she caught the scent of another werewolf. A deep, musky aroma, rich and captivating.

"What will you have?" The bartender could barely be heard over the music.

"White Zinfandel." Her words drifted through the noise, although amazingly the bartender nodded, pulling down a wineglass.

She searched the people leaning against the bar, wondering if more than one werewolf were among those pressed in around her.

A woman brushed into her, while several people tried to get the bartender's attention. Trudy held her ground though, waiting for her drink. The woman next to her did the same, offering a small apologetic smile. The beast within the lady emitted an attractive scent.

The woman had caramel-colored skin that almost glowed. Her black hair shone like silk, with tiny braids falling to her shoulders that had beads woven through them. She stood about Trudy's height, thin, with a relaxed stance, wearing a white, sleeveless mini-dress. The woman's brief glance her way allowed Trudy to see how pretty she was, with full lips and gentle brown eyes.

But her attention remained on the woman only for a second. Beyond her, at the end of the bar, a man leaned, nursing his bottle of beer and watching her. Trudy gazed back at him, mesmerized by the intensity of his green eyes. Never had she seen eyes that shade before. Maybe it had something to do with his tanned face, thick black eyebrows, and dark hair.

But it was more than coloring. A fire burned, smoldering deep within those penetrating orbs. She couldn't look away, more than aware of her reaction to his attention. Her pussy swelled, spreading heat throughout her body. The room seemed hotter the longer she stared at him. Dampness spread across her palms. He continued to stare at her, showing no concern that he captivated her with his gaze.

"Drinks are paid for." The bartender placed her glass of wine in front of her, along with the drink for the lady standing next to her.

The woman winked in her direction then glanced up and down the bar. "Who do we thank?"

The bartender nodded toward the end of the bar. The man she'd just been staring at raised his beer bottle in a silent toast. His looks improved even more when he smiled. Straight white teeth contrasted beautifully next to his tanned complexion.

"Thanks, Adam." The lady next to her returned the gesture, raising her drink before taking a sip. She turned around then, resting her elbows on the bar and watching the dance floor.

Adam. What a strong name. She offered him a nod of thanks, enjoying the cool sweetness when she sipped at her wine. He downed the rest of his beer, nodded in response then turned, disappearing into the crowd. She followed him with her gaze. Adam stood taller than most men, muscular too. Damn. She sipped again at her wine, seeking a source to cool down her suddenly fiery libido.

She needed to focus her attention on finding the couple that Elsa's mate had made arrangements for her to stay with. She hadn't expected the club they had told her to meet them at to be so crowded. And she didn't have much of a description to go by.

"Do you know Emily and Ralph Simpson?" She almost had to holler in the lady's ear next to her.

The young woman turned to face her, offering her full attention. Those soft brown eyes studied her. "Sure, I know them." She didn't smile this time, strong hesitation suddenly swarmed around her. "Do you know them?"

Trudy shook her head. The music ended, and the DJ encouraged everyone to dance to the next song. She spoke quickly while the chance remained that she could be heard. "I'm supposed to meet them here."

"Well I haven't seen either of them." The beads in her braids swung back and forth over her shoulders when she glanced over the crowd.

Her musky scent thickened, raising a question with Trudy. She didn't understand the hesitation she sensed, and now some new emotion, something she couldn't put her finger on, registered in the air. This woman didn't like being asked if she knew the Simpsons, although Trudy had no idea why.

The people around them moved, shifting or hurrying to the dance floor, when a favorite hip-hop tune began. The pretty, young black woman disappeared in the crowd, leaving Trudy standing with her wineglass in her hand.

Rick and Elsa had told her that Emily and Ralph Simpson were a few years older than she. Although she would have preferred to meet them at their home, Emily explained on the phone the day before they had plans to go out that night, and would meet her here. Emily said they would both wear red shirts to make it easier for her to spot them. And of course, they would look for her.

But she didn't see any couples wearing red shirts. The bouncer didn't pay any attention when she set her wineglass down and headed for the door. Just a bit of fresh air, and she would return to find the Simpsons.

Chapter Two

The parking lot was full of cars. It seemed every American drove wherever they went. She just wanted some fresh air, and moved to the side of the building, hoping to avoid departing drunks.

"Couldn't you find your friends?" The man spoke again, although this time the masculine scent of a werewolf drifted around her.

No one knew her plans for the evening. She was ready to demand how he could know that about her. But when she turned, her thoughts shifted in a completely different direction.

Captivating green eyes stared down at her. The man who had bought her drink for her — Adam — stared down at her. Heat flushed through her, making her mouth go dry. She ran her tongue over her lips, moistening them, while her heart skipped a beat. Were all American werewolves this gorgeous?

His gaze traveled down her, slowly, making her wish she had worn something a bit dressier. She hardly appeared sexy in her well-worn jeans and tank top. But the Simpsons hadn't told her this place was a nightclub.

He, on the other hand, made a pair of blue jeans look delectable. And the loose fitting, button-down shirt he wore, spread over a chest she would love to run her fingers across. The top couple of buttons of his shirt weren't buttoned, allowing a tempting view of curly, dark brown chest hair.

Suddenly her mouth seemed too wet.

He cocked his head, appraising her, or waiting for her to say something. Those dark forest green eyes watched her. "Are you leaving?"

She shook her head, clearing her throat. "It's smoky in there."

"You have a beautiful accent." He moved, walking to the side of her.

She wouldn't actually refer to his American accent as beautiful, so wasn't sure how to respond. But he checked her out, moving so that she stood between him and the building.

"What brings you to Fargo?" He continued with the interrogation, while taking his time looking her over.

"I'm meeting some friends here." It dawned on her that she didn't detect lust on him or any sexual curiosity toward her. She stifled her disappointment, realizing her petite features, with her plain, long blonde hair must not impress him. "I'm going back inside."

"It's still smoky in there." He sounded amused.

"Well it doesn't appear I'm going to find my friends out here." She knew she sounded a bit snappy, but it was hard to hide her disappointment that such a sexy man had no interest in her, and now was mocking her.

Strong fingers wrapped around her arm when she turned to leave. His hand was big enough for his fingers to completely encircle her arm. She wanted to rip her arm from his grasp, challenge him right there. But the emotions she smelled on him already indicated he wasn't attracted to her; no reason to make it worse by showing her aggressive side.

"Tell me who you are looking for?" His soft-spoken words caressed her, doing nothing for the fire burning inside her that she had not yet been able to put out.

His touch scorched her, the roughness of his skin against hers making it hard to remain still.

"Take your hand off of me." She wanted him to do anything but that, so kept her gaze on those long fingers, unable to look him in the eyes, knowing he would see her desire if she did.

He didn't let go.

Her heart pounded so hard it hurt, pumping blood through her body too fast, making the beast within her stir. The beat pulsed straight through her to her pussy, cum soaking her jeans.

"What are you hiding from me, little bitch?" he whispered, pulling her toward him, instead of letting go.

The muscles in his arm bulged. She imagined he used very little of his strength on her. It took a bit of effort on her part however to maintain her footing, and not stumble into him.

"I don't even know you." She yanked free of his grasp, making her arm sting where he'd gripped her. "There is no reason for me to tell you anything."

Something didn't make sense here. The best thing to do was get away from him, and ignore the need screaming through her. Americans were a bit more wild, less sophisticated. That was what she'd heard, at least. She'd always thought that was prejudice, old hogwash speaking, but it would explain this werewolf's behavior at the moment.

She turned to see several humans walking toward the club doors, paying no attention to her. He grabbed her before she could take a step in their direction.

This time he grabbed both of her arms, pressing them against the side of her body. Her breasts pushed together, offering a nice view of cleavage. His eyes lowered to the sight, and those beautiful green eyes darkened.

He lifted her, placing himself between her and the entrance to the club. "Allow me to introduce myself. I am Adam Knight."

She didn't miss the interest in his eyes, which made her wonder if he were an expert at concealing his emotions. Maybe he was trying to pick her up. Either way, he needed to learn some manners.

Fire burned in his gaze when she struggled until he let go of her arms. Her breath came almost in pants while she glared at him, intent on making him see she would not be bullied into submitting.

"Is this how all Americans say hello?" If he was trying to pick her up, that would explain his aggressive manner.

"Not all of them." He grinned, apparently finding her amusing once again.

"Just those who need a leash, huh?" She tried to walk around him, but he blocked her path, this time reaching for her face.

His fingers caressed her cheek, the warmth of his touch making her lightheaded. "It seems to me that a leash could be better used on unescorted bitches asking about werewolves they don't know."

When did he get so close to her? She blinked several times, trying to clear her head, while staring at his broad, muscular chest. His hand slid over her ear, his fingers tangling into her hair. Every time she inhaled, his masculine, earthy scent filled her lungs.

His voice had turned husky, his tone low, keeping their conversation intimate. "Now why don't you tell me your name, and why you are looking for the Simpsons?" He pulled on her hair, forcing her to look up at him.

She should fight him, not allow him to control her like this. Looking into those dark green eyes was a mistake. Damned if she could remember her name at the moment.

Her breathing came faster when he lowered his head, his gaze dropping to her mouth. He was going to kiss her! Right here at the edge of the parking lot, outside a club, with people idly moving around them. He didn't know her name, and she knew nothing about him. But he was going to kiss her!

Molten lava rushed through her, while her womb tightened. Cum soaked her cunt when his lips brushed over hers. She stifled any concerns, excitement over this sexy stranger kissing her, consuming all her rational thoughts.

"I see she is cooperating with you." A woman chuckled, the musical sound coming from right next to her.

Chapter Three

His chest was harder than a rock wall. Trudy swore her hands melted right through his shirt when she pushed against him, breaking the spell of his kiss. But his nearness still fogged her senses, muddling her thoughts.

A car drove past them in the parking lot, its exhaust filtering through the air, overriding the smell of lust and desire, which probably all came from her anyway.

The pretty bitch she had spoken to briefly inside stood next to them, grinning. Her white mini-dress clung to her curvy body, her caramel skin making the dress appear to glow in the darkness.

"Did you get her name, rank, and serial number, too?" Her laughter irritated Trudy.

"He didn't get shit." She scowled at both of them, crossing her arms against her waist.

The action had Mr. Adam Knight lowering his gaze to her breasts again. This time she wasn't daunted by his seductive behavior.

She pulled her tank top down, straightening it, realizing her hardened nipples pressed against the fabric. Let him get an eyeful. His gorgeous looks were just a cover. They were both making fun of her, and she didn't know why.

She walked around the woman this time, heading back to the club. It was time to find the Simpsons, and hopefully get the hell out of here.

"Emily and Ralph aren't in there." The pretty bitch caught her attention.

"Why didn't you tell me that inside?" Trudy focused on the lady, noticing again that some form of hesitation surrounded her.

The bitch shrugged, glancing at Adam.

"Why are you looking for them?" His question drew her gaze to him. She really needed to learn to quit looking into those sexy green eyes.

"I'm supposed to meet them here." She glanced from one to the other, while they both watched her. "Is it some kind of crime in the States to meet a couple at a bar?"

"I guess it depends on why you are meeting them." When the pretty black lady spoke, Adam gave her a quick glance, as if he didn't approve of her comment.

Americans sure were strange. Trudy held her hands out, exasperated with their cornering her like this. "Look. I just got into town. The Simpsons agreed to meet me here. I'm tired, and I would love a shower. If you'll excuse me, I'm going to find a phone and call them."

Adam reached for the phone attached to his belt, and handed it to her. After a minute of fumbling through her bag searching for the piece of paper that had the Simpsons' number on it, she took the phone. These two were making her nervous, standing there, watching her.

She dialed the number, listened to it ring several times before voice mail picked up, then left a message.

"They aren't home either." She handed the phone to Adam.

The pretty bitch ran her hand down her dress, focusing on Adam. Once again, she wished she had worn something a bit more eye-catching. She looked like a raggedy dog next to this woman.

"Where is your escort?" Was there a bit of a challenge in the woman's tone?

Trudy didn't detect anything on either of these two that made her feel she could trust them. Unescorted bitches were sleazy, and usually up to no good. But maybe these two saw that she wasn't like that. Maybe they were just trying to help her.

"She doesn't have an escort."

She was about to tell them just that. But his guess, leading to the implication that he'd already decided what type of bitch she was, made her look bad. Frustration pooled in her gut. She'd been so excited to get out and see the world all by herself, put the atrocities of her past behind her, and see what it got her. Adam probably wasn't attracted to her because he thought her a common whore.

"Where, or who my escort is, is none of your damned business." She threw her hands up in the air then let them fall, slapping her hips.

"You don't have to get so defensive." The woman cocked her head. "We're just trying to help you. Don't you want our help?"

"Help me?" She was going to lose her temper at this rate. "If you were trying to help me you would have told me the Simpsons weren't in there. All I've detected on you is hesitation since I first asked you about them."

This was good. She would end up in a fight with complete strangers her very first time alone in the States. Some time out was needed here. Time to regroup. Apparently, the warm bed and hot shower weren't to be had. She had little money, and wouldn't be able to access her account until she found a bank, which she couldn't do tonight.

"Thank you both so much for your help." She didn't bother to hide her sarcasm. They had made her mad.

Marching around the two of them, she headed toward the side of the building, needing space from people for a while. Fargo was a good-sized town. She would have to walk a bit before she could allow the change. Maybe that would be time needed to cool down so she could figure out what to do next.

"Wait a minute." Adam was following her.

She glanced over her shoulder, seeing the intent look in his eyes. The pretty bitch hurried alongside him, her curvy figure swaying all too nicely in her close-fitting dress.

Instinct kicked in. She clutched her purse to her side and took off in a sprint. She wasn't sure if she needed to run from them, or not. But the nature of her beast, the *lunewulf* breeding that pumped through her veins, had her running before she thought about it.

She hesitated at the end of the back lot. Planted trees lined the edge of the property with a busy street after that.

A vise-like grip wrapped around her waist, pulling her backward, slamming her backside against a brick wall. Adam grabbed her. He pulled her to him, knocking the wind out of her when she smacked up against his chest.

"Not so fast, little bitch." His breath brushed against her cheek, warming her insides and making it even harder to breathe. "You need to answer some questions before you go anywhere."

"Let go of me." She struggled. In fact, this time she fought him. "You can't just hold me like this. It isn't right."

Her purse strap slid down her arm, and she gripped the purse, swinging backward, aiming for his face. Her aim wasn't off.

His grip loosened, and she twisted free then bolted toward the street. But he was too close. She landed on the ground with a thud, letting out a very unladylike grunt when he landed on top of her.

"Do you really want some concerned citizen to call the local police?" He grabbed her arms, flipping her over before she could resist, like she could if she wanted to. "Do you like humans that much, little bitch?"

His eyes were as dark as the night sky, his gaze hooded and smoldering. He'd moved to the side of her quickly, at least thoughtful enough to know his weight could crush her. Although that barely gave him rank on the gentleman scale. But his chest still pinned her down, crushing one of her breasts against him. He gripped her hand with his, possibly guessing she might try to strike him again.

But he was so close, his face mere inches from hers. Dark brown hair bordered his face. His expression was grave, watching her, waiting for her reaction.

"Get the hell off of me right now." She didn't dare move a muscle. If she felt one more inch of his body touching her, she would fill the air around them with lust.

He moved to his knees, pulling her up with him. He didn't let go right away, but held her in his arms. That sultry gaze of his stole her breath, her heart pounding so hard that it hurt. Her hands pressed against his chest, and more than anything she wanted to spread her fingers, trace the rigid muscles underneath his shirt.

"Why did you run?" He was too close, his breath stealing hers when he spoke.

She forced herself to swallow, her mouth almost too dry to speak. Her entire body leaned against him, her knees off the ground while he held her. When he stood, her body slid down his until she felt the ground under her shoes. Her insides seemed to have turned to putty on her, making it hard to stand.

"Why did you tackle me to the ground?" She needed to stay mad, remember how out of line he was, or she might beg him to do it again.

He brushed dirt and grass off of her, running his hand down her side. He reached for her face, but she couldn't take it anymore. Her insides burned, her pussy cramping with an ache that hurt with its intensity.

"I'm just trying to clean you off." The slight grin on his face matched the gleam in his eyes. "I wouldn't have tackled you to the ground if you weren't headed like a damned fool into the street."

A car pulled up behind him, and someone pushed open the passenger door. Trudy saw the pretty bitch in the driver's seat.

She didn't like the looks of this. The woman looked at the two of them expectantly. Trudy let go of Adam's wrist, backing away from him.

"You're mighty skittish." He grabbed her again, turning toward the car. "Let us take you to wherever it is you are in such a hurry to get to."

She didn't have anywhere to go. And she thought she had more or less made that clear when she told them she was supposed to meet the Simpsons here.

"Thanks anyway." She pulled against his grip. "I don't need a ride."

"I think you do." He picked her up, and pushed her into the front seat, climbing in next to her.

She was pinned in between the two of them.

"What the hell is going on here?" She couldn't fight them in such close quarters. "Let me out of this car right this minute."

Chapter Four

Adam had never known the ride over to Margo's house to take so long. If he sat next to this adorable little bitch much longer he would make an ass of himself. He had a feeling already that Margo would not let him live down how he'd acted around this blonde sexpot so far.

"Let's go." He pushed his car door open the second Margo put it in park.

"John should be home soon." Margo headed toward the house in front of them, looking damned good in that white dress she'd chosen to wear tonight.

She unlocked the door, flipping on the light in the living room while Adam instinctively glanced around. Their blonde guest still hadn't said a word, possibly trying to figure her way out of being captured so easily.

He had his hesitations about her. In all his years of sniffing out criminals, she didn't fit the bill. But he was more than willing to admit she had been a distraction since he first laid eyes on her. Not very professional of him, he'd admit it. And he knew he would have to. Margo would be sure to mention his behavior to John the first chance she had.

"You want a beer, Adam?" Margo kicked her heels off, leaving the shoes on the floor by the couch. "I need to call John, let him know what is going on."

"Yeah. A beer sounds good." His blonde captive didn't fight him when he led her by the arm toward the kitchen, following Margo.

He was more than aware how soft and warm her skin was under his grip. Her fragrance, warm and tangy sweet, had him in a semi-hard state. A beer would do him good. His cock would do all the thinking for him if he weren't careful.

"What about her?" Margo turned, holding the refrigerator door open, and smiled at the blonde. "Should we let her drink?"

He wouldn't mind loosening her up a bit. "Sure. If she wants anything."

"What do you want?" Margo's gentle brown eyes strolled down the lady next to him. "Oh. That's right. You like wine."

His little blonde bitch took the chair he offered her without making eye contact. The back door was locked, and he twisted the rod on the blinds, closing them, while Margo poured wine. The chair scooting across the floor, caught his attention. By the time he'd turned around, the blonde had bolted from the kitchen.

"Damnit." She had the front door open by the time he'd made it to the living room. "Get your ass back here."

Margo yelled something from behind him, but he didn't pay attention to her. Long blonde hair flew around the little bitch in front of him, while she tore across the yard. Damn. The bitch could run. He tackled her, just before she hit the street.

"Get the hell off of me." She squirmed underneath him, his cock springing to life painfully against the softness of her ass.

She must have felt it, because she froze. He didn't have all of his weight on her; he would crush her if he did. He used his free arm to flip her over underneath him. Pale blue eyes burned with fury, her blonde hair fanned over her face. He brushed the strands aside, noticing her breath catch when he stroked her face. He knew women — knew them well. And this one was as attracted to him as he was to her.

"I'm going to start thinking you like me being on top of you if you keep bolting from me like that." The little whimper that escaped her lips sent fire through him. He needed to get off of her now, or he wouldn't be able to stand up.

Margo hurried out into the yard, stopping next to them. He'd never had a problem with a lady watching, but Margo would report to John, and he had a job to do.

"Should we tie her up?" Margo looked worried.

Adam barely managed to stand when his little blonde went into a frenzy, kicking and twisting, her blonde hair flying around her.

"Let me go. I have rights and you two will pay dearly for this." Her fingernails dug into his arm, her nails extending apparently from her fear.

He detected her temptation to change, feeling her heartbeat accelerate against his arm while he held her. "If you change into your fur, precious bitch," his body hardened, the beast within him quivering for release at the thought, "I will change too. And I think you know I will act on instinct in my fur. So behave, unless you like the thought of a rogue werewolf fucking you."

Margo laughed. "You are absolutely evil, Adam."

"Oversized mutts like you who need to bully a woman just to get a piece of tail do nothing for me." She kicked him hard in the shin, her face dropping to his arm like she would bite him.

"Whoa, sweetheart." He was glad Margo had turned toward the house. His actions were growing less and less professional by the minute. He grabbed that silky blonde hair, saving his arm, then lifted her, tossing her over his shoulder. "If I'm not turning you on, then maybe it's Margo who appeals to you."

Margo disappeared into the house, and he took advantage of the moment to give his tempting blonde bitch a good swat on the rear. "Because darlin', I can smell how aroused you are."

She yelped, sounding anything but hurt by his actions or his words. With all the frustrations of having been sent here to work this investigation, this was one moment he truly enjoyed.

"Put me down." She almost flipped off of his shoulder before he steadied her then let her slide down the front of him. "You ill-bred mutt!"

Margo walked into the living room, giving the blonde a cautious glance. "That was John." She gestured with the cordless telephone. "He'll be here in a minute."

"And who the hell is John?" The blonde backed away from him, hugging herself, her cheeks flushed a beautiful shade of pink.

"John is my mate and pack leader." Margo didn't like the blonde's tone. The last thing he needed was two bitches going at it. And he knew Margo could get mouthy when she got pushed too far.

"And is he going to bother to tell me why I've been kidnapped?" The blonde turned her attention on Margo, her hands going to her hips. "You know, I know a couple of pack leaders myself. And they won't be pleased at all when they learn how I've been treated here."

"Oh, do you?" Margo took a step forward. "And did they send you here? Did you know you were walking into the hands of FBI when you entered that bar?"

The blonde looked stunned, her arms falling to her side. She glanced at him, and then back at Margo. "Maybe you two need to tell me exactly what is going on here."

"Maybe you need to tell us what you are doing here." Margo's eyes gleamed black, her caramel skin flushed.

"That's enough Margo." He would have preferred to keep his cover a bit longer.

But the flare in his sexy blonde bitch's pale blue eyes held his gaze. Wonder and curiosity stemmed from her. There was no fear. He didn't sense panic or any other common emotions when a criminal learned his true identity. This was interesting. Maybe she really didn't know anything. Or maybe she was better at hiding her emotions than he was.

"Why don't you tell me your name?" He took advantage of her lapse of anger, hoping she would offer a bit more information about herself.

"Trudy." She continued to study him, running her tongue over her full lips. The action made his dick stiffen. She glanced at Margo, and then gave him her attention. "I'm Trudy Rousseau."

The front door opened, John entering, surprise crossing his expression immediately. "Hello." He nodded toward Trudy.

"Trudy Rousseau, this is John Campbell, pack leader in the Fargo area." He made the quick introductions, watching Trudy the entire time. Her outrage seemed to have ebbed a bit, curiosity swarming around her now. He still didn't detect any fear on her.

"Trudy was at the club asking about the Simpsons," Margo offered.

He met John's gaze, seeing the troubled look in the man's eyes. John's gaze moved to Trudy. Interest sparked, and he couldn't blame the pack leader a bit for noticing how damned sexy the blonde was.

"Margo tells me you were supposed to stay with the Simpsons."

Trudy nodded, her beautiful blue eyes watching John warily.

John headed toward the kitchen. "Put her in the spare room upstairs. Knight, you'll have to move to the couch."

"But—" Trudy started to protest, but stopped when John turned to face her.

The werewolf had a way of staring people into silence—a commendable trait.

"Miss Rousseau. The Simpsons disappeared last night. While you are visiting my pack, you will have a roof over your head." He stroked Margo's braids. "Go get her room ready for her."

Chapter Five

Margo had changed from her slinky white dress into one of her silk slips. This one had large flowers on a black background, accenting her caramel-colored skin nicely. She was a damned good-looking woman.

Chewing on the end of his pencil, Adam watched her put dishes away, his thoughts drifting to the blonde upstairs.

"She is pacing like a caged animal." John turned from the staircase, patting Margo on the rear end before opening the refrigerator. "So you think she is part of the pack involved with the humans?"

"It's a possibility. Did you get her to tell you anything?"

John joined him at the table. "She's pretty pissed off at the two of you." He grinned, looking up at his mate.

"I thought Adam might fuck her right there outside the club." Margo's brown eyes sparkled with amusement.

John pulled her onto his lap. "You would have loved watching that, wouldn't you?"

Margo's grin said it all. He had learned quickly staying with these two how sexually open they were. And John didn't seem to mind at all encouraging his mate in front of him.

"I saw how you looked at her." Margo nibbled John's ear, arching when he ran his hand over her breast. "I bet you wouldn't mind fucking her either."

Something stirred inside Adam that he hadn't expected. Thoughts of that adorable blonde fucking John put a tight knot in his gut. Not that he had any claim on the woman. Hell, he didn't even know her.

John still grinned when he met his gaze. "So tell me what you think about her."

"I'm not sure yet." But he would get to know her soon. He'd already decided that.

"Well she is here. And I want to know why." John's emotions turned serious. "I've got pack members disappearing. Either they run in the night, or we find them dead. And I want it stopped."

Adam agreed. The thought that werewolves would take money from humans to betray their own kind made him sick to his stomach. It didn't seem likely that Trudy would be part of that, but he had to make sure.

Margo stood, stretching. Her nipples hardened under the silk fabric. One of the thin straps bordered the edge of her shoulder, her creamy brown skin glowing smooth, sensual looking. She traced her delicate fingers over John's bald head.

"I don't imagine she is going to be too happy locked upstairs in that room." The soft caress of her voice caught more than his attention.

John nodded, his expression remaining serious although Adam knew the man was not unaffected by the sexy woman caressing him.

"She would run if we gave her half a chance." And Adam would be damned if he let her slip through his fingers. "I'm afraid until we have a bit of her trust, we have to keep her under lock and key."

"Our house guest is from Canada." John focused on Adam while he spoke. "She mentioned a couple of other pack leaders to me, who would vouch for her. She's a widow. A little research and I found out her previous mate ran into some trouble and died for it. It appears she is trying to make a new life for herself."

"That would explain her running alone." He never really cared for that particular pack tradition.

Trudy might have lost a mate, but she was young and sexy. He couldn't imagine she met with ready approval when she'd taken off by herself. Either that or she left a pack that didn't care about her. The only other option he didn't want to consider. And that was that she ran alone because she was up to no good.

Something brought him to life later that night. Sleeping on the couch wasn't the most comfortable arrangement in the world. It didn't surprise him that the slightest noise would cause him to stir.

Sitting and moving the cover Margo had given to him, he stared around the dark quiet living room. He heard it again. A thud, muffled but distinct, from somewhere in the back of the house. Slow heavy breathing told him John and Margo were asleep.

Nothing seemed out of place. A bumping sound, quiet enough not to be overly noticeable but consistent, grabbed his attention. It had to be coming from outside.

His job required him to carry a gun, but one glance at the shoulder holster and he decided against it. This was a werewolf matter. Any human daring to become involved would pay the same price he would give to one of his own kind.

No one stirred while he walked to the kitchen. A rush of cold air wrapped around his bare chest and legs when he opened the back door. The thudding sound came again, this time louder.

Stepping outside into the chilly night air, blood rushed through him, the change consuming him enough so that he could see in the darkness. Immediately he saw the source of the noise.

Hanging from an open second floor window, Trudy looked below her, appearing ready to jump. She caught sight of him the second she let go of the ledge.

There was no time to think. He moved under her, breaking her fall. Long strands of blonde hair blinded him, her body crushing against his. Her soft rear end pressed against his arm while her long thin legs kicked in the air in front of him.

"Hold still." He barely uttered the words, unable to catch his breath. Moving quickly to catch the fool woman had him rushing to regain his balance. But the intensity of her scent, rich and full, surrounding him like a bouquet of fresh exotic flowers, made thinking straight a challenge.

Apparently being in his arms didn't faze her a bit.

"No!" She thrashed at him, her body twisting while hair flew in his face.

She wasn't a very big woman, but she had a fire about her. He exerted some effort restraining her before she began punching him. She almost managed to slap his face before he grabbed her wrist. Every inch of her pressed against him while she slid down the front of him.

"Let me go." She didn't raise her voice, obviously not wishing to draw any more attention to herself than she already had.

"You're not going anywhere."

Grabbing her other wrist, he pinned them behind her back. She struggled moments longer before stilling, her breathing coming in pants. She wouldn't look up at him, but he brushed her hair from her face with his free hand.

"You mind telling me what you were trying to do?"

She didn't answer which wasn't surprising. The tank top she'd worn since earlier now twisted over her breasts. Full round breasts slightly on the large side. Just the way he liked them. Fabric stretched sideways allowing more cleavage to show. Her nipples were hardened nubs, stabbing through the material. His mouth watered at the sight.

"You're hurting my wrists." She twisted her arms but he doubted she was in pain.

Adjusting his grip, he enjoyed the determination that forced her mouth into an adorable pout. Long lashes fluttered over deep orbs of sultry blue.

"The only thing hurting you is your pride." He couldn't hide the fact that he was enjoying himself.

She glared at him. "How dare you decide how I feel."

He didn't expect her to kick him. The sharp pain in his shin startled him. She pulled away, falling to her knees, and even managed to crawl several feet away before he caught her.

Her long legs were muscular, yet thin. And she was strong. Kicking, she fought him until he held her ankle, flipping her to her back.

"I know you don't like being a captive." He dropped to his knees, wanting to be closer to her, itching to lie on top of her.

Once again her twisted shirt distracted him, the material pulling against the firm mounds dangerously close to revealing one of her nipples.

"You don't know anything about me." She struggled furiously, almost throwing him back with the fury she applied while she kicked at him.

The only thing he could do to stop her was to cover her, using his body to pin her to the ground. The outrage in her glare should have hindered him. But she was so damned sexy, so tempting with her clothes nearly twisted off of her. Long silky strands of blonde hair fanned around her. He ached to run his fingers through them, pinning her head so she could only look at him instead of thrash about.

"Maybe I want to know more about you." There was no maybe to it.

Watching those full pouty lips pucker while she glared up at him, he ached to lean forward and kiss her. Just a few inches. Their faces were so close to each other.

But instead of insulting him, or accusing him of mistreating her, she surprised him. Her expression softened, something akin to a wounded animal drifting over her expression. When she blinked, the fury left her gaze. Those sultry blue eyes looked up at him almost helpless.

"I crawled out of the window because I have to go to the bathroom."

Chapter Six

There was no way she would let him see her cry. One moment he had the look of a lusty animal, ready to devour her. And the next compassion riddled his expression, those dangerous green eyes softening noticeably.

"You crawled out of the window because you needed to use the bathroom?" He didn't believe her, she could tell.

"The door was locked. I guess I could have kicked it open." She would never do that. But she sure enjoyed the surprised look he gave her. "Would you get off of me, please?"

He stood with an agility that impressed her for his size, pulling her right up along with him. Muscles and his masculine scent seemed to surround her. More than anything, she wanted to run her hands over his incredible body that she would swear was touching her everywhere.

Disappointment rushed through her when he didn't hold her but guided her by the wrist into the house. He didn't stop until they stood before the bathroom door. She shut the door behind her, grateful for a few minutes to regroup without him handling her and distracting her with his presence.

Her attempt at escape had proven futile. Not that she would let him know she was trying to get away. He would restrain her even further if he knew she couldn't be trusted.

She splashed water over her face, taking her time before opening the door. He stood on the other side. She could smell him. And his scent was driving her mad with lust. No amount of scrubbing would get rid of the desire she knew lingered in the air around her, not even a shower.

"Feel better?" He stood just outside the bathroom door, leaning against the wall in the hallway.

Muscles in his arms bulged, even relaxed and crossed over his chest. And what a chest. Dark, coarse curls spread over his biceps. She swallowed. Knowing he detected her interest bothered her. He stood so relaxed, the boxer shorts he wore leaving little to the imagination. And for the life of her, she still didn't detect any interest in the air around him. That made her mad. She wasn't *that* ugly. Maybe he went for the younger werewolves. But hell, she wasn't *that* old either. Thirty was still young.

And why do you care so much what he thinks of you? He is holding you prisoner!

"I feel much better. Thank you." She would march right past him and return to her cell. Okay. So the bedroom was nice and clean, and better than sleeping in the woods again, but she was here against her will.

Adam pushed away from the wall, blocking her path. She didn't look up, couldn't look up. Simply staring at that perfect chest, while his all male scent lured her, took her breath away. She balled her hands into fists, feeling the dampness on her palms. Why did he have to make her so damned nervous?

"Where did you plan on going?"

"Huh?" She thought he wanted her to go back upstairs.

"When you climbed out the window."

She looked up into those deep green eyes and her knees went weak. Hints of gold streaked around his irises. The corner of his mouth twitched, almost as if he hid a smile.

"I told you," she began, wondering how he knew she really had tried to escape.

He raised his hand, stroking her cheek. Her heart raced while her body temperature soared to dangerous levels. His fingers wrapped around her neck, squeezing just enough so she couldn't speak. One finger pressed against her jaw, lifting her head. Pushing her against the wall, the cold hard surface doing nothing to soothe the fire burning inside her, he moved closer.

"And that will be the only time you lie to me." His face was inches from hers. The heat from his body adding to the fire burning within her.

Everything around her was Adam Knight. His strength held her against the wall while his gaze pinned her, seizing her heart, capturing her breath. The world around them disappeared while the pounding of her heart began to match the throbbing deep inside her pussy.

The corner of his mouth twitched again, satisfaction brimming in his gaze while his hand lifted her jaw, raising her face closer to his. He knew how his actions affected her, the confidence in his eyes confirming that.

His lips brushed against hers before she could catch her breath. The right thing to do would be to put him in his place. Regardless of his strength, his incredible good looks, he shouldn't be able to turn her into a liquid state of lust with a simple touch. At this rate she would be begging him to fuck her within minutes.

"You can't just…" She tried to tell him that he had no right to kiss her like this.

His lips pressed against hers, stealing her words. The softness of his mouth contrasting against the power of his grasp made it hard to think straight. No man had ever turned her on so quickly, made her crave him so much. She tried to turn her head, needing to moisten her lips, regain control of the moment. But his fingers tightened around her jaw, keeping her mouth where he wanted it.

His tongue met hers, rushes of fire swarming from his kiss, melting her insides. She gasped, unable to help herself. This shouldn't be happening. Her mouth opened to his and he growled his satisfaction.

Oh God. Moisture brimmed inside her pussy, the swelling growing painful. She ached to press against his body, feel the hardness of him against her.

His mouth tore from hers, leaving her gasping for breath. Turning her head with his fingers pressed against her jaw, her neck exposed to him, he left a hot moist trail across her cheek with his tongue. He scraped his teeth over her sensitive flesh and she cried out.

Gasping, she fought for breath. "Stop. You can't do this."

She reached for his wrist, trying to pull his hand from her face, but he grabbed her with his other hand. Ignoring her plight, his hand slid down her arm, until he brushed against her breast. Explosions of liquid heat flooded through her when he squeezed her, then ran his fingers over her nipple.

"Damnit," she hissed. An orgasm ripped through her, taking her strength with it. She collapsed against him while fisting her hand against his chest, wanting to pound him for making her so weak.

His fingers pressed against her tummy, pulling her shirt up, exposing her breast.

"Perfect." His breath was hot against her flesh.

Latching on to her nipple, he sucked her into his mouth, his teeth grazing over her, currents of electricity ripping through her. Blood boiled through her veins. Her bones popped and ached to grow into something stronger, fiercer, more aggressive. He controlled her feelings, physically and emotionally, and she didn't like that. She wanted to be in control.

Grabbing his shoulders, she squeezed the hard muscle, barely able to stretch her fingers over them. Adrenaline rushed through her, bringing the change to life without her bidding. Strength to stop him, push him away from her, ebbed at her fingertips. Women of breeding never changed into werewolves inside a home, especially someone else's home.

Adam growled—a growl too low for any human to make. The vibration seared through her skin, branding her with his heat. He warned her though, letting her know he sensed her change, her craving, her desire for something more than her human shape could offer. Her scent had aroused the beast within him.

This could get really dangerous.

"You've got to stop. Please." She hated how she sounded helpless, at his mercy. The sound of her own voice made her cringe.

He straightened, lifting his head, towering over her. He didn't lower her shirt however, his large hands continuing to caress her tortured flesh. Gold streaks heightened the intensity of his green eyes, which devoured her. Tousled brown hair fell in strands around his face, making him look even sexier. If that were possible.

"You don't want me to do this anymore?" He kneaded her breasts, tugging and squeezing. The warmth from his touch spreading through her, igniting a fire deep inside her.

She opened her mouth to speak, her lips moving but no sound coming out. Staring into those passion-filled green eyes would make her forget her name.

"You want this." He rolled her nipples in between his fingers and thumbs. "More than anything, you want this."

She should tell him to go to hell. Give him a good kick in the "you know what". Enlighten him on how he was not in charge of her. Yes. She should do all of those things.

But when he knelt before her, nipping at her belly while his fingers grabbed the top of her shorts, fire rushed through her with so much intensity she worried she would pass out.

The hardness of the wall did nothing to brace her when he tugged on her shorts, the material sagging to her ankles with little effort.

"Damn, woman." His breath burned right through her.

Pride rushed through her that he liked the sight of her shaven pussy. His lips captured her heat, while his tongue darted over her sensitive folds, finding her throbbing clit.

"Holy shit." She bit her lip, closing her eyes while his tongue stroked her cunt.

Adam kissed and licked, exploring her pussy with his mouth. It didn't matter anymore that he had taken the upper hand with her. She would teach him later how to behave. Right now all she wanted was for him never to stop.

He dipped inside her, the roughness of his tongue stroking her just inside her pussy. White sparks danced before her eyes. She itched to grab his hair, thrust herself against his face, force him to devour her until she exploded.

But if she moved she feared she would fall over. Already her legs seemed wobbly. He grabbed her inner thigh with one hand, spreading her legs apart further. She almost fell forward, grabbing his shoulders to stabilize herself. His groan sent shivers through her.

Her world capsized. Rushes of liquid heat, fiery hot, broke through the pressure built in her womb. She came with more intensity than she ever remembered doing before.

Apparently she bit her lip because she tasted blood. Opening her eyes, everything blurred around her. Adam Knight had just given her the best orgasm of her life. He kissed her pussy with enough tenderness that it was almost too much to bear. Never had her strength been depleted from her so thoroughly. And that scared her to death.

"Let's put you to bed." He stood, filling her space, seeming to sense her state of being without her having to speak.

She almost leaned into him. But glancing past him, she caught a glimpse of John Campbell before he turned and moved silently back up the stairs.

Chapter Seven

Trudy toweled dry then grabbed the clothes she had worn the night before. Just pulling the shorts up over her legs brought back memories of what she'd done with Adam. A wave of humiliation washed over her.

"I don't know who you think you are, Adam Knight." She didn't know whether to be angrier with him or herself.

Steam washed around her when she opened the bathroom door, stepping out into the cool hallway. It had surprised her to find her bedroom door unlocked this morning. But then to find that the house appeared to be empty confused her further.

He slept on the couch last night. He could still be there.

The smell of coffee recently brewed encouraged her down the stairs. But she didn't smell any food cooking. Maybe they all had jobs.

"Good morning." Margo lowered the newspaper she'd been reading. She sat at the kitchen table, her long bare legs stretched out in front of her. Dark red nail polish made even her feet look good. "Help yourself to coffee."

Even with a hair wrap, and no makeup, Margo had an erotic sense about her. Trudy combed her fingers through her wet hair and pulled a coffee cup from a hook under the counter.

"Thanks." She wanted to know where the men were. And if Margo knew her mate was a peeping tom.

Cold sweat dampened her palms at the thought of John watching Adam get her off the night before. Her own state of mind had been so tormented she guessed that was why she hadn't detected him on the stairs. And she wouldn't even ponder how long he had been there.

Sitting across from Margo, she blew on her coffee. "Am I no longer a prisoner?"

"Adam told me to tell you why we brought you here—what we believed." Margo folded the paper in front of her. "And what is going on with our pack."

A wave of sadness appeared in Margo's expression. Maybe last night had an impact on Adam deciding to enlighten her. The coffee tasted good, bringing her to life while she waited for the woman across from her to continue.

"Where is he now?" She didn't want to ask, hating the fact that she couldn't keep the question to herself. It didn't matter where Adam was, as long as he wasn't here.

"John is at work. He's a reporter for the newspaper, covers local interest pieces." She smoothed her hand over the folded newspaper, the dark red fingernail polish matching the polish on her toes. "And Adam is off doing whatever it is he does. I'm not sure."

Margo shrugged, meeting her gaze. Her caramel-colored skin didn't have a single blemish and long black lashes fluttered over her soft brown eyes.

"I just wondered." Warmth traveled through her, which had to be from the coffee.

"When you mentioned the Simpsons last night I thought you might be one of the werewolves tipping off the humans."

She put her coffee cup on the table, staring at the woman across from her. "What the hell are you talking about?"

Margo smiled. She stood, the long T-shirt she wore hanging on her like a dress. She opened the refrigerator and pulled out a plate with foil over it. "Adam told us this morning that he didn't think you were involved with them. That's why he wanted me to explain to you why we brought you here. Last night we weren't sure. And with the Simpsons disappearing yesterday, well things looked a bit suspicious."

"The Simpsons have disappeared?" But she had just talked to them.

"There is an organization of humans who are trying to wipe out werewolves. I can't imagine what their line is, but they have managed to get some of us on their side. These werewolves are paid to turn their own kind over to these humans." Margo pulled the foil off of a couple steaks on the plate. She stuck it in the microwave and pushed a few buttons. It hummed to life. "Once the humans know for sure they are tracking werewolves, they come in and kill them."

Trudy couldn't believe what she was hearing. "Who would help humans do this?"

When Margo turned around, the outraged look in her eyes stole some of her beauty. "Some very sick werewolves, that's who."

Adam must have decided that since she wasn't guilty of some crime she could stay or leave. Obviously he'd had his fun with her, let their pack leader get an eyeful, and that was it. Realizing she wasn't as wise to the ways of the world as she thought she had been, she swallowed the bile of humiliation that rose in her gut.

The microwave beeped and Margo pulled the plate out with the steak on it. "Do you want some of this meat?"

She shook her head. "Will I be chased down if I take a walk?" Fresh air sounded real good at the moment.

"It's hard saying what Adam might do." The hardness in Margo's expression softened when she grinned. "I think he'd like it if you stayed here. He's putting the moves on you, you know."

Trudy shrugged. There was no reason to make a big deal out of any of his actions. "By the looks of him, I'm sure he's just a womanizer."

Margo brought the plate and a fresh cup of coffee to the table. "He's damned good-looking. You're right about that. But he's been staying with us for a few months now and he's never brought any women around. When he's not working, he is here. I don't think there are any women in his life."

So she wasn't in a line of many. Or at least, not any that Margo knew of. Either way, there was no reason to make a big deal out of what happened the night before. Adrenaline had peaked. That was all.

She might as well continue with the plans she'd made for herself, when she thought she would be staying with Emily and Ralph Simpson. More than anything she wished for clean clothes to put on before she left the house. If her bag was still where she left it when she arrived in town the night before, she would have clothes.

"Please feel our home is your home." Margo's gentle brown eyes added to the sincerity in her tone. "And let me know if you need anything."

The last thing she wanted to do would be to borrow any of Margo's clothes. As sexy as the woman was, Trudy knew none of Margo's clothes would look good on her. Leaving the house, she walked several blocks before getting her bearings. The smells of the city made it harder to track where she had been the night before. More than anything, she didn't want to stray into a part of the town that was predominantly human. She'd never been real comfortable around them. A being with only half a soul, unable to change into the beast that offered a true release of emotions, they made her wary. After hearing what Margo said about some of them being aware of werewolves in the area, and out to hunt them down, she hoped this part of town was predominantly werewolves.

A bank and a convenience store were across the street. A pack leader wouldn't live in a neighborhood overrun by humans. Hopefully there would be at least one werewolf working at the bank who could walk her through accessing some of the money from her trust fund. Hurrying across at the light, she walked through the parking lot toward the bank.

A small Toyota truck pulled in front of her, stopping her in her tracks.

"Going anywhere in particular?" John Campbell rested a well-developed arm on the top of his rolled down window. Black eyes strolled down her, easily making her stomach flip-flop.

He'd watched her explode last night, seen her cry out with her orgasm. A trickle of excitement over that fact caused goose bumps to travel over her skin. She tossed her hair over her shoulder, frustrated with her reaction to his gaze. He was mated and he'd been out of line. Grossly out of line.

"I'm going to the bank. I need to see if I can access my trust fund." The only reason she told him this was because he was pack leader. Otherwise she would have told him to go to hell.

John whipped his truck around, pulling it into the nearest stall. "I'll walk you in and see that Harold talks to you."

She would have told him he didn't need to do that, but he was already out of the truck and escorting her to the bank. After opening the door for her, he pulled his cell phone from his belt and punched in some numbers. It only took a minute for her to realize he spoke with Margo. Leaving her in the waiting area, he disappeared around the corner.

"Harold will help you with anything you need," John told her when he reappeared with a stocky older man. "And Margo will be here in about thirty minutes. If you want to do any running around, she'd be glad to take you."

His dark eyes, black as night skin, and towering size, would make him hard to challenge. She wondered at her own intelligence when she felt like telling him she didn't need a babysitter. Bothered by the fact that he managed to keep her quiet with a look, she turned away, nodding.

Morning turned to afternoon and Trudy couldn't deny that she'd had a good time.

"Is there anywhere else you want to go?" Margo helped arrange bags in the backseat of the car.

After making arrangements to access some of her trust fund, Margo had taken her to where she had left her bag of clothes the night before. Both of them agreed the night air and dampness made everything in the cloth bag unsuitable until washed. So they had gone shopping.

"Well I'm starved. How about you?" Trudy shut the back door of Margo's car then slid into the front seat.

"Marinated chicken on the grill sounds good to me."

Margo didn't say much while they walked through the aisles of the grocery store. By the time they'd unloaded all of the bags into the kitchen she began wondering when Adam would show up. Thoughts of seeing him again after last night plagued her. Even though everything about him confused her, she couldn't deny the small amount of excitement that he might be here soon.

"There's something I want you to know." Margo finished putting groceries in the cabinets and turned to face her. "I know John watched you and Adam last night."

Chapter Eight

Trudy's stomach turned into knots. Margo looked away, heading toward the living room. Even in shorts and a T-shirt the woman was elegant. She carried herself like a queen. Trudy imagined the woman held the respect of every bitch in the pack.

But she had no idea what to say to her comment. If knowing her mate had been a voyeur last night bothered her, Trudy couldn't tell. All she sensed from her was a calmness that was unsettling.

"I told him that he could." Margo turned in the middle of the living room, those soft brown eyes studying her, looking for a reaction. "John sensed that you were uncomfortable around him and he thought it best that I tell you."

"You told him that he could?" She didn't understand. Granted she was in their home, but it seemed a bit forward that these werewolves thought that gave them leave to watch such an intimate moment.

Margo walked over to the front window, possibly also wondering when the men would be home. She didn't want to be having this conversation when they walked in the door, and possibly Margo felt the same way.

"Adam has been living with us for over three months now. He's a very sexy man, irresistible in some ways. Don't you agree?"

Since Margo knew she'd fooled around with him the night before, she didn't see why she should comment. Obviously he knew how to turn on a woman. Her heart began pounding while unease settled in her gut. She watched Margo lick her lips.

"I want you to know that I love John with everything I have." Margo turned, pinning her with her gaze. The seriousness in her expression made her appear like she thought she would be challenged. "I would kill for that man. And I have."

She nodded. Often the queen bitch fought for her mate. The woman's gaze didn't falter, but Trudy didn't back down and continued to stare back. She'd done nothing wrong. In no way had she approached John, and no explanation needed to be offered on her part. She would let Margo say her piece.

"Shortly after Adam started staying with us, John asked me if I would let him watch us have sex. I agreed and it was such a turn on knowing he was in the room while John fucked me. I loved it."

She imagined Adam watching Margo and John. They were a very attractive couple. Margo tugged on her T-shirt, once again staring out the front window. The material stretched over her willowy body, accenting round firm breasts. Her legs were long and thin. Everything about the woman declared elegance and class. She didn't doubt Adam would have been turned on seeing her naked and being fucked.

Knowing that the three of them shared this intimacy spread awkwardness through her. She swallowed, doing her best to sound calm and not allow her reaction to fill the room with its scent.

"Did Adam know that John was going to watch?" She felt like the outsider here and more than a bit used.

Margo nodded.

The urge to turn and march out of the house raced through her with such fierceness that she tightened her muscles, forcing herself to hold her ground.

Trudy heard the car pull into the drive out front at the same time that Margo's body stiffened. Turning from the window, she walked toward her, her look showing she refused to feel bad for anything she had just shared.

"Adam is a good man. I can see that you are interested in him." When Margo walked past her, she paused, placing her hand on Trudy's shoulder. "You have my blessing."

John coming home changed the atmosphere and the conversation. He and Margo chatted about pack business while busying themselves in the kitchen. Having nothing better to do, she sat at the table listening. Even during dinner the two of them communicated like a truly bonded couple. Finishing each other's sentences, laughing at their jokes, Trudy could see how well mated they were.

"You've sat here silently through most of the meal." Margo helped John clear plates when none of them could eat another bite. "Tell us about you. Why did you leave your pack?"

She watched Margo make a plate and cover it with foil, more than likely supper for Adam whenever he got home. The woman probably viewed both men as hers to some extent. Jealousy trickled through her, an emotion she despised. Forcing her thoughts on the conversation, she reminded herself that she had no room to be jealous. In no way did she wish to lay claim to Adam Knight.

"I'm a widow," she began, deciding sharing a bit about her past wouldn't hurt. "After my mate died I wanted to make a go of it on my own. I left with my pack leader's blessing."

John nodded. "Then you shall have widow status."

"I appreciate that." Widow status allowed her freedom she wouldn't have as a single bitch. No one would question her living by herself or running by herself.

The back door opened and Adam walked in, bringing the chilly night air in with him. Car grease and body sweat surrounded him.

"Good God. You're a mess." Margo wrinkled her nose.

"And hello to you too." Adam tugged at one of her braids. "I promise I'll shower before eating."

The familiar gesture, a closeness between the two of them, couldn't be missed. John's attention riveted to Adam, but he didn't appear concerned about the way he touched his mate. Once again she felt like the outsider, watching the intimacy of a close family. But this wasn't a family. And this man had almost fucked her last night. His attention toward Margo, before he noticed her, didn't sit well.

"Where have you been?" John asked.

"I headed up to Grand Forks and visited with some of the werewolves in that pack." Adam ran his hand through his hair, messing it up.

"Did you figure out which werewolves were running information?"

John's question grabbed her attention. Margo stopped stacking dishes, turning toward the men. Trudy glanced from one of them to the other, her gaze resting on Adam.

He looked her way, his expression haunted. Chills rushed through her when she imagined what he might have learned today.

"Your source was right. She was blonde, petite and pretty." Adam didn't look away from her while he spoke. "Hopefully we stopped her before she relayed any more information."

"Where is she?" Margo asked.

Adam didn't answer. Instead, he walked past her, heading toward the stairs. "I need a shower."

His scent drifted around her, powerful, dangerous, and all werewolf. She lowered her gaze, focusing on how his T-shirt stretched over bulging chest muscles. Her pussy swelled, the throbbing growing almost painful when she realized how badly she would like to fuck him.

He had thought her a criminal when he first met her. Apparently she matched the description of a werewolf feeding information to humans. Her gut tightened at the thought. He hadn't answered Margo's question about what happened to the bitch they had been looking for. Somehow, last night she'd shown them she wasn't who they thought she was. But if she hadn't, Adam might have killed her. Something must be wrong with her. Even the thought that he had the power to overtake her, kill her or fuck her, still made her wet with desire for him.

It took a minute to realize the phone had been ringing for a while when she woke up later that night. Moonlight streamed through the parted curtains. She rolled over, wondering why no one answered.

Her skin itched while her bones ached to pop and grow. Chasing rabbits and enjoying a good run might be just what she needed. Padding toward the stairs, she paused until she heard the steady breathing of sleeping coming from John and Margo's bedroom. The stairs didn't squeak, which was probably why she hadn't noticed John the night before.

"Tonight might not be the best night to run alone, little bitch."

Trudy jumped, not noticing Adam until he approached her from the darkness of the living room.

"I can take care of myself." She turned toward the back door when Adam's fingers snaked around her arm.

The heat of his touch sent sparks racing through her.

"I'm sure you can." His voice was deep and rumbly. "But I would prefer you not to be out alone."

Turning, she gazed into those dark green eyes, glowing with lust while he stared down at her. She hadn't realized John was awake too until he appeared behind Adam, the cordless phone in his hand. Long black lashes hooded his black eyes, which looked more than interested.

Chapter Nine

"You are not my keeper." Her heart raced while his green eyes darkened.

"Maybe you need one." He pulled her to him, the feel of his muscular chest like steel against her palm.

"You thought me a criminal last night." She didn't know why she pushed the matter. Holding her as close as he did, his gaze dark, penetrating, he didn't look like a man to be crossed.

"I had my suspicions, yes." His expression didn't change. Fine chiseled features offering no indication of his thoughts, except for his eyes.

She wanted to know his thoughts, longed for some indication of what he thought of her. All she had to go by were those dark green eyes. He never looked away from her, but probed deep into her gaze. She feared if she didn't blink, or look away, he would know her every thought.

Breaking eye contact, she focused on his neck and the wisp of dark hair that curled right at his collarbone. She spread her fingers over the warmth of his chest feeling his heart race against her palm. The hard beat matched the pounding of her heart. That same pulse inflamed her pussy, making it swell and ache for attention.

John moved behind Adam, catching her attention. She watched him hang up the phone. He turned, meeting her gaze, those black eyes intense and serious.

As if Adam wanted her attention on him, he released her arm, snaking his fingers through her hair. He gripped, pulling close to the roots with a quick tug. Having her hair pulled by him turned her on more than she would ever admit.

He turned her head so their gazes locked. "Pay attention to me." His command showed his possessive side.

Her breath caught in her throat, his desire to be the focus of her attention brought her heart to a complete standstill.

"Okay." All she could do was whisper, but it was enough.

She saw the sparks flame to life deep within those dark green eyes. There was no way she could say no to him; she wanted him too desperately. Now she had just told him as much.

She swore a smile appeared, but she couldn't focus. His lips seared hers before she had a chance. Fire rushed through her. Suddenly her heart beat way too fast. Blood rushed through her veins. The room grew warmer, she would swear to it.

His lips were moist, the heat from his kiss spreading a fever through her. She wanted to kiss him back, needed to have more of him. Tingles shot through her hands when she brushed her palms over his skin, gripping his shoulders, holding on for dear life.

"Damn." She gasped for air, hardly able to catch her breath when his mouth left hers.

"I need you," he breathed into her neck, nibbling at that sensitive spot next to her collarbone.

His fingers were rough against her skin, but his touch gentle. He tugged on her shorts, loosening them with little effort.

She should stop him. Opening her eyes for the briefest of seconds, she focused on John, leaning against the doorway. He stroked his cock through his shorts, the large thick shaft outlined clearly through the material.

Adam's mouth moved to her breast, his teeth grazing her nipple through the material of her T-shirt.

"Dear God." She cried out, realizing Margo would hear her if she weren't careful.

Did either of them care if John's mate knew what the two of them were doing? This warped threesome confused her, but her mind was in no shape to ponder the matter.

"Tell me what you want." Adam's demand seemed to come to her from miles away.

She worked to calm her breathing, her pussy throbbing with such intensity while blood rushed through her faster than her human form could handle. Focusing on his words, and trying not to pay as much attention to his mouth on her breast, she tried to think of how to answer.

The words came from her before she could give them thought. "Fuck me."

His chuckle against her tormented flesh sent chills through her. Her favorite pair of shorts that she slept in every night, slid down her legs. She found no resistance in her when Adam pulled her T-shirt over her head, leaving her naked in front of him and John.

Excitement mixed with a pang of guilt deep in her gut. Moisture clung to her pussy, her nipples hard and eager to be sucked. Adam straightened, reaching for his shorts while he focused on her.

"You are so fucking beautiful." He smiled, his green eyes sparkling in the dark kitchen.

"She's gorgeous." John's comment alerted her to how relaxed he was, as if he belonged there, being part of this even if just as a voyeur.

When Adam stepped out of his shorts, her mouth went dry. Smooth skin stretched over his thick long shaft while his round, swollen cockhead beckoned her. He walked into her, pressing her against the counter. His cock throbbed into the soft part of her belly. The hair from his chest tortured her nipples. As he wrapped his arms around her, she molded into him, enjoying feeling him against her like this.

Lust hung thick in the air around them. This time, his kiss was more aggressive, his tongue fucking her mouth. She ran her fingers through his hair, enjoying how silky it felt. She would have explored every inch of him, become more familiar with his body, but her body demanded satisfaction. Lifting her leg, wrapping it around his waist, she wanted him to know that she needed him now.

He pulled his mouth away from hers, grinning. "Are we anxious?"

Fire rushed through her when he teased her.

"This is your fault. You started this." She dug her fingers into his shoulders, wanting his body lower, his cock nearer to her inflamed cunt.

His grin didn't waver. "And I will finish it." His hand moved between them, his fingers gliding down her until he cupped her pussy.

Licking her lips, she couldn't look away. Her mouth seemed too dry, then too wet. Feverish heat made her blood boil in her veins. She struggled to breathe while he parted her swollen pussy lips, spreading her thick cream around her clit.

She glanced over at John. He stroked that oversized cock of his, his breathing almost as tormented as hers.

Adam thrust deep inside her, almost knocking her off her feet. She took it as a silent reminder that her attention needed to remain on him.

"Damn, woman. You're tight as hell." He didn't sound like he was complaining. "And absolutely soaked."

If he expected conversation at this point, he would be sadly disappointed. She met his gaze, breathing through her mouth and trying not to pant. Never had she imagined fingers stroking the inside of her cunt could feel so damned good.

"You need this, don't you, my sexy little bitch." He pulled his finger out, stroking her hard, throbbing clit, and then pressed his way deep inside her.

"God. Yes." She could hardly stand. He built a pressure inside her with each thrust.

She wanted to let her head fall back, to collapse into him and ride his fingers. But she wouldn't let herself get out of control. John watched them. And she had a feeling she was being used to return a favor. She had to keep her head on straight and take this for what it was—casual sex.

And what if Margo finds out about this little escapade?

Her body language must have somehow betrayed her thoughts because he pulled his finger out of her and reached for her. Strong hands ran down her back, giving her chills.

"I can tell how badly you want me." His words brushed over her tortured skin, giving her a rush that went straight to her toes.

He turned her around, the cool counter doing nothing to soothe her feverish state of mind when she leaned against it. Obviously he hadn't wished her to respond. He began nibbling on her shoulder, his large hand smoothing down her back.

She couldn't help herself. She arched into his touch. Sticking her rear end out, she exposed her soaked cunt to him. His cock pressed dangerously close to her throbbing hole, and she closed her eyes, willing him inside her.

"All that matters is me." He must have realized she was nervous about John watching.

She nodded. More than anything she wanted him inside her. John watching seemed a bit strange to her, she wouldn't deny that, but she would worry about that later.

His knuckles brushed against her rear end, while his cockhead probed closer to her cunt. She shifted, doing what she could to help ease his entrance.

She sucked in her breath when his bulging cock began pressing inside her. Further and deeper, he stretched and filled her. Pressure built more and more, the deeper he penetrated. Her cunt throbbed while her juices soaked them both, the moisture clinging to the inside of her legs.

"Dear God. Adam." He kept moving into her further and further, as if he grew even more while inside her.

She gripped the counter, arching further into him, certain if he filled her any further he would split her in two, but loving the sensations that rippled through her.

His hands gripped her hips, rough and hard. "Damn, baby. My cock loves your pussy."

"Yes." She couldn't manage speech.

His cock teased her insides, caressing her while he pulled out, and then glided back in. "Tell me how you want me to fuck you."

His comment startled her, but only for a moment. Matthew had never cared how she wanted to be fucked. Everything had been about his pleasure. Adam made her feel better at that moment than he would ever know.

"Hard and fast. Fuck me until I tell you to stop." She tried to see him over her shoulder. "And don't come until I tell you."

She thought she saw him grin, but didn't have time to focus when he slammed into her.

"Oh. Shit." She held on to the counter for dear life.

She could feel his balls slap against her while he rode her harder than she'd ever been fucked before.

"Is this how you want it, baby?"

She nodded, her hair falling around her face, unable to speak while the heat soared inside her cunt. The friction building between them sent waves of heat through her. Holding on to the counter like it was her lifeline, she gritted her teeth, determined to ride out the pressure that threatened to explode at any moment. The orgasm of her life was about to happen, and she wanted to enjoy every second of it.

His grunting behind her let her know he was enjoying this too. He held on to her hips so tightly she wondered if she wouldn't be bruised in the morning. It didn't matter. He fucked her so damned well she would endure anything, and wasn't about to make any comment that might make him stop.

"I'm not sure how much longer I can go."

"Not yet." She shook her head, tossing her hair out of her way.

His cock thrust deep inside her, almost knocking her over, hitting a point that sent her over the edge. Almost falling over, she cried out, feeling the dam break, her orgasm rippling through her while cum seeped out of her pussy, dripping down her legs.

He didn't miss his cue. Hitting her deep inside one last time, his hot cum shot inside her, burning her with its intensity.

When she would have collapsed against the counter he reached for her, those powerful arms wrapping around her.

"Better now?"

She nodded. "Perfect."

Chapter Ten

Her skin was moist with sweat when she collapsed against him. There were a few after-trembles. Adam felt them when he lifted her into his arms.

"I'm taking you up to bed." She didn't argue, but cuddled against him, like she belonged there.

Something tightened inside him, a reality that he liked the idea of having her there. Refusing to give it any thought, he turned his attention to John. Margo cuddled up next to him, her face glowing like she'd just been the one fucked.

"We'll talk to you two tomorrow." John nodded to both of them.

Margo remained huddled into her mate, her nightgown a bit twisted on her. She focused on Trudy though. She had been with women before, but since he didn't know how Trudy would feel about that, he'd told them all they could do tonight was watch. Both of them were so excited to have her included in the intimacy they shared with him. But something inside him wasn't ready. Sex with Trudy and Margo sounded fantastic. That wasn't it. He wanted to know Trudy better, learn more about her first.

After doing a search on her, and learning about her pack giving her three mates, he knew she'd explored group sex before. Whether she had enjoyed it or not, he didn't know. But when he read about her previous mate, killed by his pack after committing murder, instinct kicked in. Trudy ran from a nightmare. She needed protection.

She mumbled something when he wrapped the blankets around her, savoring her smooth warm skin while he brushed his knuckles over her cheek.

"Sleep tight, beautiful."

She didn't answer. He hadn't expected her to. He stood watching her though, until her breathing slowed, enjoying how the moonlight streamed in from the partially closed windows and made her blonde hair look like silk. He'd never met anyone like her — so delicate, yet so feisty.

The covers draped over her, showing the curve of her breast. If she had still been awake, he might have tried to fuck her again. Hell, he knew he would have. His cock danced at the thought. But he had a feeling she'd played the cocky role earlier to impress him, make him think she could handle anything.

Smiling, he backed out of the room, knowing he could watch her all night. Unfortunately, sleep didn't come as easily for him. Muffled sounds behind John and Margo's door told him they weren't asleep yet, either. He could go in there. They would let him watch. Hell, he could probably fuck Margo too if he wanted. He and John had shared her on more than one occasion.

But that didn't interest him tonight. Trudy's scent clung to him and he was in no hurry to let it go. Walking through the silent house, he let himself out the back door.

The night air wrapped around his naked body, sending fierce chills through him instantly. He closed his eyes, allowing his heart to pump faster, feeling the blood rush through him, warming him, while the change took over.

Dropping to all fours, he could see clearer now in the darkness. Stretching his powerful body, he took only a moment to enjoy his heightened senses before taking off in a full run.

He didn't have to think about where he was going—he knew. He headed home. Once a week or so, he tried to make it back to the small town on the edge of the Badlands where he'd grown up. Hickory wasn't on most maps and few people knew it was named after the founding werewolf who settled the area. It didn't have the malls that Fargo had, or the nightlife.

But he'd made a vow to always call it home.

You are an alpha male without a pack. Protector of all packs. His father's words rang through his memories, as they had many times before since his death. *An alpha must be stronger, more powerful, with a stronger instinct to protect. Not many pack leaders could hold the rank that you hold.*

Reaching Highway 2, he angled off, veering toward the north, and home. For some reason, he wondered what his father would have thought of Trudy. *It would take a strong woman to walk alongside you.* He knew his father had never said that, but he could imagine him saying it. *Stronger than a queen bitch, she would possess the power to make them belly up to her.*

The sun bordered on the horizon, while morning dew soaked his coat. It didn't wash Trudy's scent from him though. Thoughts of her tight pussy, the way her muscles clung to him while he had fucked her made him wish he had stayed in Fargo. He loved how soft and silky her skin was. The way her long hair drifted down her back and fell around her face made him itch to grab a hold of it. And those soft blue eyes. His blood warmed when he thought of how they sparkled to life when she challenged him. Everything about her turned him on.

But there was more to her than just a sexy body. Granted, she was pretty damned hot. The fact that she had left her pack, sought out a new life unescorted, and had made it this far unscathed told him something about her. She was tough, able to take care of herself, and willing to take on others. That was one hell of a good quality in a woman.

The isolated ranch house came into view and he slowed to a stop. Sitting in the wet grass, he realized he'd been running for several hours now. Panting, he took a moment to catch his breath while taking in the beauty of his land. All of it was his.

The sprawling brick house below, with his two-car garage and one outbuilding, nestled on the edge of the Badlands, had been everything his father had. And he proudly left it to Adam, his only cub.

Someday you will leave it to your cub. His father had been proud of this land.

Turning, he walked up hill a ways, stopping at a group of bushes. Pulling on some overgrown grass with his teeth, he brushed the growth away from the simple grave marker. His father wasn't buried there. Werewolves held strong with the tradition of cremating their dead. But this had been his father's thinking spot, and his ashes were spread over this ground.

You would have liked her, Dad.

The sun slowly warmed his damp coat, reminding him the day had begun. He turned from the grave marker and trotted down the hill. He needed a hot shower.

At his front door, naked and sweaty, he punched in the security numbers to disarm the alarm system. The series of beeps following told him it had already been disarmed.

"Hi, boss. It's me." Raven Moore, the young werewolf the Bureau had assigned to him several months ago, swirled his office chair around when he strolled into his living room. "Damn. You smell. Get yourself a piece of tail last night?"

"She's not a piece of tail." He ignored her sitting in his dining room, which instead of a dining room table housed computer and surveillance equipment, and headed for the bathroom.

After being up all night, a good nap should be in order, but he would settle for a hot shower, and then there was work to do.

He lathered soap over his chest, almost hating to wash away Trudy's scent. Thoughts of her bent over the counter, her adorable ass so soft to the touch, had him hard as a rock. Grabbing his cock, he stroked it, imagining her beckoning him.

"I want you to fuck me." He could hear her soft voice in his head.

Everything about her turned him on. Her petite features with breasts large enough to grab a hold of and nipples that were made for his mouth. That silky blonde hair of hers felt so damned good when it stroked over his skin, tickling and arousing all at the same time. Those sultry blue eyes, challenging him and submitting to him. No female from any pack he'd worked with had ever affected him the way she did. He should be terrified.

The water ran over him while he rubbed his shaft. Pressure built inside him, craving her, missing her already. He ran his fingers up and down his cock, feeling the blood pump through him. More than anything he wanted to fuck her again, feel that tight pussy around him. Her cries of pleasure echoed in his head. She had loved what he had done to her.

His pulse pounded through his cock. He could feel it against his fingers. Gripping harder, he stroked his cock, the urge to come building. He licked his lips, remembering how she tasted, how sweet her shaven pussy was pressed against his mouth.

"God. Damn. Woman, you are in my system." And he wasn't sure he wanted her out.

The steam from the shower seemed to intensify around him, closing in on him. His hand was a weak substitute for what he'd discovered in Trudy. But for the moment, it was the best he could do. Spilling his seed into the shower, he leaned against the shower wall, waiting for sanity to return to his brain.

"I've got a stack of articles for you. I had them faxed over here. They are from newspapers around the state." Raven nodded to the copies on the long table pushed up against the wall, when he strolled into the room, showered with clean clothes on. "You aren't going to like them."

Adam walked barefoot into the kitchen, needing just a minute before he read bad news. He was grateful that Raven had a full pot of coffee waiting for him.

Nothing he read set well with him. Article after article claimed sightings of oversized wolves, speculations of werewolves, and actions cities were taking to try and exterminate these dangerous creatures.

No werewolf would attack a human, under any circumstances. And he'd heard of no case of where anyone had. Nor had he heard about werewolves running in packs through towns. If that had happened, measures would be taken immediately to prevent those werewolves from doing that again. Usually pack leaders were allowed to handle rogue werewolves on their own. He only stepped in when matters accelerated beyond the pack leader's capabilities.

"This one is my favorite." Raven moved so she pointed over his shoulder, her tone disgusted, and pointed at one of the faxed articles. "'Farmer Single Handedly Wipes Out Monsters.' The whole thing pisses me off."

He couldn't agree more. Scanning the article, his stomach churned when he read the interview of a human who proudly showed off several corpses laying in his yard. The article covered half the page, explaining how these beasts could take the form of humans to trick their prey.

"We've discovered the only way they can be killed is by breaking their necks. This makes sense since they have no heart. They're cursed by the devil," the human was quoted as saying. "But some of them know they are cursed and have told us how to find the others."

Local authorities assured the reporter that they anticipated all of these beast humans, whom that reporter hesitated to call werewolves, would be destroyed soon.

"The humans are trapping more and more werewolves every day." Raven began pacing behind him, a trait he'd grown accustomed to. Her best brainstorms often came after she created a worn path in his carpet.

But he felt her frustration. It clogged the air around them. Flipping the pages to the last article, published by the pack newsletter for the surrounding counties, he read the concerns listed there.

"Actions need to be taken quickly in order to prevent more dens from being annihilated," he read silently. Discussion of a mass exodus to more remote areas was being discussed by several packs in the state.

"If we have packs fleeing the area it will draw more attention to us." He doubted Raven even heard him. She continued to pace, seemingly lost in thought.

One of the pack leaders quoted in the article said he'd placed his pack under strict orders not to run alone, or go anywhere without letting someone else know their whereabouts.

Adam's thoughts drifted to Trudy. If he hadn't woken when John answered the phone, he possibly wouldn't have been able to prevent her from running alone. But there wouldn't be anyone to keep an eye on her today while he was gone. His insides tightened at the thought of humans getting their hands on her. She would fight to the death, which normally he would view as a wonderful quality in her, but right now he feared it would be her own death. He needed to call and warn her. But would she listen to him?

Chapter Eleven

Trudy thanked the lady who'd shown her the small house and walked toward her car. She'd accomplished a lot in one day, buying a nice little used car, and making appointments to find a place to live, but she didn't feel a bit happy about any of it. Aggravation still seeped through her.

The man had a lot of nerve. He'd fucked her better than any werewolf ever had before. And now he was gone. There had been no note, no mention to John or Margo where he had gone. He had just left. She chewed her lower lip, sitting in the driver's seat of her little Honda. It shouldn't bother her that she had no idea where he was. Tell that to the annoying ball of knots that wouldn't leave her stomach.

Adam was a mystery. Maybe that appealed to her as much as his sexy good looks. Disappearing without even the pack leader knowing where he went. Not to mention, he was FBI. She didn't even know there were werewolves in the predominantly human bureau.

"Are you going to sit here and daydream all day?" she grumbled, glad no one was around to hear her. It wouldn't help matters any if the new bitch in the pack was discovered to blank out every now and then, lost in her own imagination.

The section of newspaper she'd taken with her, folded neatly with the ads circled that appealed to her, rested on the seat next to her. There was no point in dwelling on matters she had no control over. All she could do was take care of herself. And right now she needed to find a place to live.

Pulling into the driveway of John and Margo's home several hours later, she wished she had somewhere else to go. Nothing was working out the way she wanted it to. She stared at the peaceful house with its clean yard and simple exterior while butterflies danced in her stomach. Both of them had watched Adam fuck her last night. And she hadn't been able to read Margo's expression when Adam had carried her upstairs.

Those strong arms had wrapped around her, lifting her like she was no more than a child. He was so strong, so tall and well-built. And his cock. Damn. Her pussy craved him inside her again already.

He could get so hard, so thick, so long. And he knew how to fuck her, hitting just the right spot over and over again. Her pussy began throbbing. She would end up masturbating right here in the driveway if she didn't quit thinking about him. Those penetrating green eyes wouldn't leave her alone though. It seemed he watched her, his gaze pinned on her, even though no one knew where he was. The thought of it was unsettling.

By the end of the week, Trudy knew she couldn't spend another night in John and Margo's house. Listening to them fuck every night, imagining John doing to Margo what Adam had done to her, was about to make her nuts. She'd learned of a boarding house run by werewolves on the other side of town. That afternoon she reserved a room.

And it was a damned good thing the room came furnished. Plopping her one little bag down on the ruffled bedspread that covered the single bed, a wave of loneliness swept over her.

The older female who ran the Inn had told her she had just the room for her. Frilly pale green curtains hung over the two windows in her second floor room. The carpet beneath her was thick, and other than her single bed, a strong implication the innkeeper didn't approve of single bitches having overnight guests, she had a bureau and a desk. Running her finger over the well-polished surface of the bureau, she wondered for the hundredth time this week where Adam was.

Someone tapped on the door and hope leapt through her. It was all she could do to hide her disappointment when Margo entered. Of course Adam wouldn't knock gently on a door. He'd probably enter like he owned the place.

"This is a nice room." The queen bitch glanced around at the furnishings, smiling when she met Trudy's gaze. "Are you sure you want to stay here? You know you are welcome in our home."

She couldn't very well tell the lady the sounds of her and her mate fucking every night were making her crazy.

"I came here to start a new life." She hoped her smile was sincere. She meant what she said. "You've been kind to welcome me into your den. But I need to establish a home of my own."

"And this is it?" Margo's warm chuckle was contagious.

"No. This isn't it." Looking around the small room, it looked like anything but home. Maybe a motel room. Albeit a cozy, well-furnished room.

Margo reached for her bag that she'd placed on the floor when she'd entered. Moving over to the desk, she sat down and pulled out a bottle of blood-colored wine and two small plastic cups. Trudy sat on the edge of her single bed, hoping she appeared relaxed.

"Well, we'll toast to your new place anyway."

Over the past few days, while Adam had been gone, Margo had made quite the effort to be nice to her. It was hard not to warm up to the bitch. She'd grown accustomed to her natural beauty and charm. And it was hard not to be friendly to someone who seemed so intent on seeing to her needs.

There really was no reason to be upset with the knowledge that Adam had shared intimate moments with Margo and John. He'd disappeared out of their lives too, even though Margo had told her he'd done this before. Trudy knew she wouldn't be able to have a relationship with a man who took off without a word. So it was best he had disappeared before she'd become more involved with him. At least she hadn't become emotionally attached to him.

Then why do you fantasize about fucking him every night?

Margo allowed her teeth to grow enough to use them to pull the cork from the bottle. It released with a fizzy pop. She poured the dark liquid into the two glasses and offered one of them to Trudy.

"To your happiness." She lifted her own cup, offering the toast, while her soft brown eyes seemed to probe, seeing emotions Trudy would rather keep to herself.

"And to yours."

Sipping the wine in silence, Trudy wished she was more comfortable around Margo. Everything about the woman showed perfection. Knowing she'd seen Trudy naked, watched her experience orgasm after orgasm, had heard the sounds she made when she came, made her feel more than exposed in her company.

"This is good wine." Margo licked her lips and Trudy decided it might be better to stare out the window. Even in baggy old jeans and a plain brown T-shirt, Margo had a seductive edge about her. "I wish I could say I picked it out but Adam bought it last week."

Just hearing his name made her heart pick up speed. "Should we be drinking it then?"

"Sure. He knows I love wine and brought it home. I just hadn't had a chance to drink it yet. I thought it would be nice to share it with you."

"This is very kind of you." She would not allow herself to feel jealous because the man bought Margo a bottle of wine. All it showed was he had a relationship with Margo and not with her. Which was fine.

Margo shrugged. "I like you." She finished off her glass and poured more wine, standing and filling Trudy's glass then sitting on the bed next to her. "But I get mixed emotions from you. John told me that you had three mates in your old pack. I guess I assumed group sex appealed to you when I shared how Adam had joined us. Maybe I shouldn't have."

It made sense that John would have contacted her old pack. She didn't know what to say about group sex appealing to her. "I didn't ask to have three mates. It was pack law."

"Mighty fine law." Margo chuckled into her glass while sipping more wine.

She didn't feel like digging up old ghosts. It would be hard to explain to someone who loved being with more than one man at a time how the law had its bad sides.

"It had its moments." The best thing to do was to make light of it. She sipped at her wine, its rich smoothness helping to calm her insides.

Margo turned on the bed, facing her, her expression serious. "I want you to know that I think Adam likes you. He's never brought any women home since he's been staying with us."

He didn't have to. He had you.

She stared into the pool of dark crimson in her cup. Her heart weighed heavy when penetrating green eyes appeared in her mind. Knowing hands, so strong yet so gentle, with his body an image of perfection. She ached to run her hands through his hair, hear him whisper her name. Just allowing thoughts of Adam made her pussy throb, her breasts ache, and her nipples harden. What she wouldn't do to know where he was right now.

"Maybe I'm sensing your emotions wrong." Margo reached out and stroked Trudy's hair away from her face. "But I think you miss him."

Her heart leaped from an extra beat when Margo touched her. She hadn't expected that. The softness of her fingers and long fingernails gently brushing against her gave her chills. More than anything she wished she'd worn a bra that day. Her nipples poked through her shirt like eager beacons aching to be played with.

Margo leaned forward, placing her cup on the bed stand, then taking hers and doing the same. A trickle of sweat beaded between her breasts, betraying her when she would have hid her nervousness. When Margo straightened she sat a lot closer than she had a minute ago. Trudy studied her perfect caramel-colored complexion, how her long black eyelashes fluttered over her brown eyes, and those naturally dark rose lips formed a perfect heart shape.

"Don't be nervous," Margo whispered, this time running her fingertips over Trudy's hair.

She stiffened in spite of herself. Lust drifted ever so slightly in the air around them, the faintness of its scent teasing her senses.

"What are you doing?" She didn't know why she whispered anymore than she understood why her pussy seemed moister than it had a moment before.

"You are just so incredibly sexy." Margo leaned forward, brushing her full lips over Trudy's cheek. "Ever since I watched Adam fuck you I've imagined what you would feel like."

It had never occurred to her that Margo would be bisexual. She wondered why it surprised her. Maybe because being with another woman had never crossed her mind. She'd heard stories over the years about other women playing together. And she had never judged someone for his or her personal sexual preference. It just wasn't something she'd ever thought of trying.

Margo ran her fingers along her jawbone, her face mere inches away. Her scent was musky, alluring, a certain temptation to anyone attracted to her. She wondered if John knew she was here, and if so, what he would think of what she was doing.

Margo's fingers glided past her cheek and down the front of her shirt. Fingernails scraped over her nipples, sending a rush of chills straight to her pussy. She shivered, her pussy swelling in response to the evocative touch.

"I've never..." She couldn't finish when Margo brushed her lips over hers. Her words got lost on a gasp, a flood of desire filling the air around them.

"But you want to," Margo whispered into her mouth, deepening the kiss.

She didn't know if she wanted to or not. Her thoughts spilled over each other, distracted by how her body was reacting to this unexpected seduction. Margo pressed her palm into Trudy's breast, flattening it, her nipple crushing against the warm skin through her shirt.

Thoughts of Adam touching her like that invaded her senses and it took a minute for her to realize she was kissing Margo back. Her pussy throbbed, pulsating as rapidly as her heart. But her mind dwelled on Adam, not the beautiful and sexy woman caressing her at the moment.

Margo slid her fingers under Trudy's shirt, the heat from her touch scorching Trudy's senses. Lust filled the air around them. And she knew it was a mixture of both of their emotions. Goose bumps danced over her skin while Margo's fingers glided against her tummy. She had a hard time believing a woman could make her feel so aroused.

Breaking the kiss, she moved inches away, fighting to control her breathing. It took a minute before she looked into those sensual brown eyes, noting the desire swimming in Margo's gaze.

"I think you are a hard woman to say no to." Her voice sounded too husky. She tugged on her shirt, her body in turmoil from desire and confusion over what might happen here any moment.

Margo smiled, perfect white teeth making her dark complexion glow. "I thought you might like this."

"I do." She'd be a fool to deny her arousal. Margo could smell it in the air around them as easily as she could. "But…"

She almost cried out when someone knocked on the door. Without waiting for an answer, John opened the door, his massive frame suddenly hovering over them.

"We've just interrupted a meeting between two werewolves and several humans." He didn't bother with introductions.

The seriousness in his tone had her jumping to her feet, guilt at being caught in an almost compromising position flooded through her in a cold sweat.

"We've got them locked up. I want you to round up all the females." He glanced from one of them to the other. If he realized what he just interrupted, he gave no indication of caring.

Margo stood with enough grace to make Trudy feel like a fool for being so skittish. "I'll need an hour or so to contact everyone. Where are you holding them?"

"We've turned Ralph and Emily's home into a holding cell, since it's empty right now." He pulled Margo into his arms, kissing her tenderly on the forehead. Then looking over her, his gaze met hers. Dark eyes, sparkling like onyx, softened when he looked at her. "You're under my protection, Trudy. I want you to stay close to Margo. I promised Adam I would take care of you."

Then turning, he left the room, leaving a world of questions swarming in her head.

Chapter Twelve

Adam tossed his cell phone onto the passenger seat. John Campbell's words didn't sit well with him, but the message hadn't been a surprise. Taking the exit off the highway, he slowed into traffic. He hadn't been to Fargo all week and thoughts of seeing Trudy brought his cock to life. Adjusting in the driver's seat, he tried to make room in his jeans for his growing hard-on.

He'd met with most pack leaders in the northwest over the past week. They'd worked around the clock tracking leads, and narrowing in on the werewolves leaking information to humans. In spite of the intensity of the meetings, he'd never been able to get Trudy far from his thoughts.

He craved the sweet taste of her pussy, the softness of her skin, the rich sweet scent that seemed to surround her no matter her mood. She'd gotten into his system and he planned on getting inside her as soon as he could.

Fargo had turned into a good-sized city over the years, but he still seemed to know the roads like the back of his hand. Turning the corner toward John and Margo's home, his cell phone beeped and he reached for it while pulling into their driveway.

"Hey boss." Raven's soft voice sounded worried. "I've just heard word that there is a pack of humans planning a raid on what they think are a bunch of werewolf homes."

"Humans don't form packs." He was ready for this to end. If he had no contact with humans for the rest of his life he would be a happy man.

"Whatever." Raven sounded tired of it all, too. "I am working on details. Are you in Fargo yet?"

"Yup." He let himself into the Campbell home, the silence making it clear no one was here.

"Well, I'm headed that way too. I've got a list of homes they plan to raid. Seems they think a bunch of accidental fires might do the trick."

"I want to know where they will meet before they plan their attack."

"I'm working on it. I'll call you when I get down there." She hung up without saying goodbye, another one of her traits he'd grown accustomed to.

He grabbed his cell phone again when he reached the upstairs spare bedroom only to find it empty of any of Trudy's things.

"Why didn't you tell me Trudy moved out?" he barked into his phone the second John Campbell answered.

"She moved into Polly Marshall's bed and breakfast a couple days ago. Margo has attached herself to Trudy. We're keeping a close eye on her for you." Although John also sounded tired, he detected a bit of amusement in the werewolf's tone.

"How close of an eye are you keeping on her?" The thought of Trudy screaming with pleasure for anyone other than him got his dander up.

John laughed. "Not that close. Although I think Margo has tried a time or two."

Margo was a damned nymphomaniac. John seemed to enjoy that quality about her which was all that mattered. But still, he didn't want the bitch messing with Trudy. Well, maybe if he was there to watch. Otherwise, he didn't want anyone touching her. All they were supposed to do was ensure her safety.

"Where are you now?" He really wanted to know where Trudy was, and to go see her. Maybe if he could see that she was okay he would be able to focus on matters better.

"We're over here at the Simpson place. I've got a couple of terrified humans locked up in one of the bedrooms. The smell is nauseating. They aren't talking though. Your help would be appreciated."

Adam growled. The situation had escalated beyond his comfort zone. Humans being kept in a den. What would happen next?

"I'm on my way over." He took another look around the vacated bedroom. "Where is Trudy now?"

"I'll contact Margo and let you know."

It bothered him knowing Trudy was out and about with Margo. The woman might be queen bitch, with duties to perform, but Trudy would do better by his side, where he knew she would be safe.

Back in his car—he was beginning to think he lived in the damned thing—he headed into town to meet John. After a minute he realized he was looking twice at every car that resembled Margo's. Trudy would be with her, and he needed to see her. Granted, he couldn't wait to sink his cock into that tight pussy again. Feeling her soft skin against his, her breath tickling his senses, all of that had his heart pounding. More than anything the sound of her crying out his name, knowing that he was the one who could please her like no other werewolf would ever be able to, had his blood rushing through him. He needed to remind her how well he could fuck her.

This young bitch, a widowed werewolf, had strolled into his life and turned everything upside down. None of it made any sense to him. Stopping at a red light, he watched a group of human teenagers stroll across the street. They should be in school. If humans spent more time focusing on improving their own, instead of worrying about werewolves, everyone would be happier.

And he would be a hell of a lot happier if he could spend his days napping with Trudy instead of talking to humans. Damnit. The woman would not stay out of his thoughts.

"Find her and fuck her," he mumbled. Maybe then he could take care of matters at hand.

The Simpsons had an older home. Trees offered lots of shade for the neighborhood and blocked the houses, making it hard to see addresses. He recognized John's Honda parked on the street and pulled up behind it. Getting out of his car, he listened to the sounds of the neighborhood, getting a feel for the place, before approaching the house.

John opened the door for him before he could knock. "I think we've made some headway," he said in form of greeting.

"Bring me up to date." Adam glanced at the other werewolves in the living room.

He didn't know many of John's pack but displeasure weighed heavy in the air. Nothing could cover up the smell of the humans though. They were beings with half of a soul, an incomplete creature. The stifled smell of so many emotions kept locked up with no true release was an unpleasant odor. Some werewolves didn't mind it. And he knew in the past his kind had mingled with humans. But it had never been for him.

"I think we have a name of one of their leaders. Apparently they claim this human hunts werewolves and pays other humans to bring dead werewolves to him."

Adam watched John's jaw twitch. The werewolf fought for control. Frustrated anger was barely detectable on the man. He'd give him credit for keeping his emotions in check. Unlike these poor humans, John would be able to enjoy a good run later tonight, releasing the unpleasant emotions. But maintaining control when needed was a sign of a good pack leader. And John Campbell was one of the better leaders he'd dealt with.

"Do you know where this human is?" Adam looked down at the piece of paper John handed him.

"He isn't from around here, making him out of my jurisdiction." John's expression showed he would love to take the human down himself.

Adam nodded, taking the piece of paper. "Since this is your territory, I'll let you decide what to do with the humans."

He knew John wouldn't kill them. It wasn't in his nature. Just like it wasn't the nature of most werewolves to take aggressive acts with humans. They were a weaker species. There was no glory in the kill of humans, especially when you couldn't eat them. That would violate every pack law throughout the world to do such a thing.

"Looks like I need to pay this human a visit." He looked at the address, noting it was at least a four-hour drive north of here.

"Are you leaving town right away?" John followed him to the door.

He couldn't leave town before he saw Trudy. He would go nuts if he did. "The sooner this ends, the better for all of us."

Walking to his car, he knew he hadn't answered the pack leader. But then he also guessed John knew he would seek out Trudy.

Chapter Thirteen

The night air rippled through Adam's fur. He tore the ground with extended claws, running as fast and hard as he could. His breath forced through him, pooling around his face like steam from a locomotive train. Nothing stopped him, tall meadow grass flattening in his path. Forcing his speed up the rocky hill did nothing to calm the fire burning within him.

He couldn't find Trudy. The Bureau wanted to know why he hadn't left already to seek out this human werewolf hunter. His day had gone to hell.

Sensing another werewolf, he turned his head toward the smell. But that was it. If someone wanted to run with him, they better be in damned good shape. He wasn't in the mood for a lazy stroll under the star-filled sky.

Raven appeared in the tall grass, running as fast as her smaller frame would allow. Her brown fur, similar to his, made her a blur in the night. But she was breathing loud enough to wake the dead. He gained a small bit of satisfaction in knowing she had to work hard to find and catch up with him. Let her suffer. There wasn't anything she could tell him right now that would cheer him up.

Slow down, damnit. She growled at him.

Get in better shape. If she didn't like his mood, she could find someone else to run with.

Raven didn't complain further, but did her best to keep up. He was sure she had some update. Or maybe she'd been assigned to accompany him when he visited the human. None of it mattered. He wasn't going to do a damn thing until he burned off some steam. She fell in alongside him, or more like right behind him, not attempting to growl her disdain but keeping quiet. Damn good thing, too.

A noise caught his attention. Something moved through the prairie grass. All he saw was a white blur, and it was moving faster than he'd ever seen a creature move before.

Raven turned her head toward the noise—a werewolf, smaller than she was, and as white as the moon. Raven's hackles went up but she didn't have time to prepare for the attack.

Adam jumped to the side to keep the two women from tumbling into him. Snarls and loud growls violated the air. He jumped onto both females while they were rolling around on the ground, separating them with a quick snap of his teeth.

What the hell is going on here?

Raven ducked behind him, able to move and growling, so obviously not hurt too much. The petite white werewolf bared her teeth, prancing defiantly, egging Raven on. Raven would have none of it, not that it surprised or bothered him that she wouldn't fight over him. She held her head up high, still growling, and then strutted off, leaving him alone with the outraged female by his side.

And although he'd been taken back for a moment, he knew who had just offered to fight for him. And he was more than willing to claim his prize now that Raven had left them alone. Staring down at Trudy, watching her quick breathing, while her slick coat almost glowed in the darkness, his cock hardened, eager to dive deep inside her.

Moonlight reflected in her silver eyes, sharp teeth still bared while she focused on Raven's parting figure. He wasn't too worried about his assistant. He would catch up with her later. More than likely she would chew his ass over the matter, but she would get over it. What had his heart pounding a mile a minute was that Trudy just challenged Raven because she thought they were running together.

Mine!

Primal instincts demanded that he claim the offerings of the winning bitch. Prancing to the side, he would dance the dance of the desired male, while impatiently waiting for her to offer her belly.

He no longer heard Raven, and obviously neither did Trudy. Her body relaxed, fine tuned muscles moving under her glossy coat. Her expression calmed, the anger floating around her dissipating. But then she turned from him. *Wait a minute.*

He moved in closer, reminding her that he was ready and waiting. Surprised, he almost jumped back when she turned on him, snarling and snapping. Once again her teeth bared. She lowered her head, her ears flattening, while she ordered him to stand back.

She was so close to the ground he could step over her with little effort. But this beautiful white creature now had the nerve to turn and tell him how it was going to be.

You are the one who just lay claim to me, sweetheart. He kept his rumble low in his throat. There was no reason to scare her.

Her ears twitched while her silver eyes glared at him. He sensed no fear on her. But what struck him as odd was that if he didn't know better he would swear he smelled anger on her. No. More than anger. Trudy appeared outraged.

Lowering his head, giving them a better chance at seeing eye to eye, he moved closer. Trudy darted around him, lunging and snapping at his legs. She almost broke the skin.

She let out a series of barks, her tone more than harsh. Now the lady had a lot of nerve. He raised his head, letting her know exactly what he thought of her attitude.

If you think you can make a challenge and then walk away like this, lady...

She lunged at him. And she didn't look like she was in the mood to fuck. Damnit. The woman was attacking *him* now. Had she gone rabid?

Jumping to the side, he had half a mind to send her rolling, just to remind her of her place. The last thing he would have was her bullying him. She was out of line. After all, hadn't he been sick with worry about her all damned day long? The woman didn't account for her whereabouts, and she knew the peril surrounding them right now. Not knowing where she was had distracted him and made it hard to work. He wouldn't have her yelling at him now.

Trudy moved faster than he anticipated. Her teeth clamped down on him, scratching his side. A burning sensation ripped through him. Enough was enough.

Turning on her, he returned the attack. Not enough to hurt her, but enough for her to know he wouldn't tolerate this behavior.

She glared at him, jumping out of his way, and stumbling briefly. She recovered quickly, barking a few profanities. Then she turned and ran. Her sleek coat distracted him—shiny and white, he imagined her softer than silk. But she was also quickly disappearing. And he would be damned if she would get out of his sight.

Lunging after her, he took off at full speed, realizing he needed to apply every bit of muscle he had into his run just to keep her in sight. Damn. The woman was fast.

Maybe this was her idea of foreplay. Granted, he hadn't noticed much of a cultural difference in her, but she did come from another country. Her pack might have rituals he hadn't heard of. More than most, he was an open-minded werewolf. But this might be one of her customs she would have to let go of.

Where he had run uphill before, now he struggled with his balance while moving as quickly as he could down the hill. Trudy seemed to have no problem flying down the countryside. She was almost out of sight. He'd never known a werewolf who could outrun him before.

Thoughts of fucking her tight pussy faded. Frustration took over. Not only were they headed in the wrong direction that he needed to go, she was losing him. And he did not like to lose.

He smelled danger before he heard it. Gunfire ripped through the air. The smell of humans clogged his senses. His muscles tightened painfully while he reigned in his gait. Slowing to a cautious stroll, he moved silently through the night, sniffing the air. Humans were ahead of him, and there were a fair amount of them.

Worse yet, someone had fired a gun. If Trudy was hurt, none of them would live through the night.

She almost ran into him before he saw her. White fur tumbled forward, barely stopping in time before they collided. Her growling whimpers showed her fear. Well at least she wasn't hurt, and she had enough sense to know to return to his side when she smelled danger.

More gunfire riveted through the air. Trudy pressed against him. They could hear humans running toward them. Their excited shouts making their mission clear.

"Werewolves! They are over here!"

Chapter Fourteen

Humans closed in around them but the creatures didn't have much sense. They were making enough noise to alert every night creature within a mile radius. Turning into Trudy, he hoped she hadn't worn herself out.

Move. Now!

There was no reason to play with these humans. They would shoot up a storm, possibly hit one of them, but more than likely kill some innocent animals and possibly one of their own.

Trudy didn't need any encouragement to run with him away from the humans. He didn't want her to think he ran from danger. But hopefully she realized he would see to her safety first. She didn't slow, but stayed by his side, all the way to his home.

Allowing the change to take over, he pushed the numbers on the security pad next to his front door. She stood naked behind him, her expression wide-eyed, showing her terror and confusion.

"You're going to freeze standing there." He stood to the side, in the dark living room, waiting for her to enter.

She walked slowly past him, turning quickly when he shut the door.

"Where are we?"

He moved past her, reaching for the nearest lamp. "Home."

"This is your home?" She turned, crossing her arms over those ample breasts, her flat tummy and shaved pussy begging for his touch.

"Yup." He would love to give her the tour, fuck her in every room, but matters needed attention.

He gripped her bare ass, guiding her toward the kitchen, leading her through the dark.

"Are we safe here?" She was looking around her, worry staining her pretty face.

There were phone calls to make, but he would give her this minute. Turning her so she faced him, he combed his fingers through her tangled hair. "You are safer here than any other place in the world."

She looked so troubled, puzzled, nibbling on her lower lip. He pulled her into his arms, knowing she wouldn't resist. She needed comfort. More than likely she'd never heard a gunshot before, or been chased like her life depended on it. Most werewolves hadn't. And if he did his job well, his kind would never know that life.

Her heart pounded against his chest. Stroking her back, feeling her relax in his arms, he realized how much she needed him. Her nipples were hard little pebbles pressing against his bare chest. The soft warmth of her body rushed through him, making his blood boil.

Even after running in their fur from Fargo to his home, she still had that sweet smell unique only to her. His cock throbbed, swollen and hard, next to the soft flesh in between her hipbones. Running his hand just over the sweet curve of her ass, he pressed her to him, torturing himself with her nearness.

"I worried about you today." He believed in honesty between two people, and would let her know his feelings.

She stiffened, lifting her face to look up at him. "Why would you do that?" Her tone sounded cold, but he understood her confusion. Most werewolves didn't open up to their mates. And if she would challenge another female for him, she must be looking at him as a possible mate.

He smiled, wanting more than anything to wipe that worry from her face. Those pouty lips beckoned him and instead of telling her why, he decided to show her.

Her lips were so moist, so hot. Dipping his tongue into her heat, tasting the sweetness of her mouth, he suddenly felt as awkward as a pup. Her erotic fire scorched his senses, sending fire through his blood and straight to his cock.

Somewhere in the back of his mind, he knew he had responsibilities, duties that only he could handle. But Trudy's kiss rattled his senses, making it impossible to want anything other than to be buried deep inside her. He rationalized that John Campbell would have called him if matters had escalated beyond his control. More than likely, the humans had given up on their chase, and now downed beer at their local hangout, bragging about what didn't happen.

Trudy ended the kiss, gasping. Her hot breath tortured his skin.

He could tell she needed him as much as he needed her. "Come here."

Reaching behind him, groping for one of the chairs at the kitchen table, he grabbed it, making it wobble as he turned it around. He could barely focus, every drop of blood seemed to have left his brain and pounded painfully in his cock.

"I don't want to…" Her words rode on her gasps.

He straightened the chair and sat down, reaching for her. She didn't hesitate but came to him.

"Yes you do." He didn't have time to think about why she would protest. If her fears had consumed her he would calm them later. But her body language clearly stated what she wanted.

Very little light came through the kitchen windows. But even in the darkness he could see how seductive she was. Letting go of her hand, he gripped her hips, guiding her over him. She straddled him, the rich scent of her pussy an aphrodisiac to his already tortured senses. Smooth and sweet, he couldn't take his eyes off her pussy. Her shaven lips parted when she stretched her legs to settle on his lap. He swore he could feel the heat of her cunt before she even touched him.

"Adam…I…" She whispered his name, while he held her hips, pulling her cunt closer to his cock.

"I want you, too." He adjusted her so she pressed against his cockhead, the heat from her burning him alive. "Dear God, baby." He wanted to watch, but the moisture clinging to her wrapped around his cock, sucking him in. Closing his eyes, it was all he could do to keep himself upright so that he could fuck her. She glided on to him like a tight glove, made just for him.

"Oh damn." She cried out, grabbing his shoulders.

He had to see her. She lowered herself onto his cock, taking over, moving slowly. When he opened his eyes, it was a struggle through blurred vision to focus on her. Long blonde strands draped around her face while she looked down. Her expression was serious, intent on her movement. That adorable mouth of hers puckered into a circle.

"That's it, baby. Ride my cock." He wanted so badly to take over, slam himself deep inside her heat.

Her fingers dug into his shoulders. Her leg muscles strained against his outer thighs, while she moved slowly and deliberately, gliding her pussy up and down over his cock.

"I will, but only if we do it my way." She shot him a quick look, her blue orbs on fire.

He saw the defiance in her expression, with a slight raise of her eyebrow. Her body shook when she lowered herself over his shaft, burying him deep inside her heat with painful slowness.

"Fuck me however you like." He reached for her breasts, squeezing them gently, enjoying how she shivered once she had him deep inside her.

She might be trying to torture him for some reason, but she wasn't unaffected by it. He ran his thumbs over the tender plumpness of her breasts, adoring the softness, while he watched her face flush with desire.

"Oh I will, wolf man." She wanted to sound cocky, but he could see how she fought to keep control.

She raised herself off of him. Her moistness clung to his cock. The heat from her pussy rushed through him. It was so hard not to force her right back down on him. He could feel her body shake. She let her head fall back, arching into him while she lifted off of him.

"Shit. Oh. Shit." The muscles inside her clamped around the head of his cock and she dug her fingernails into his shoulders.

"That's it, darlin'; soak my cock." She was making him crazy. If he held still a moment longer he was sure every blood vessel inside him would explode.

He squeezed her breasts, her nipples puckering eagerly in front of him. Taking one of them into his mouth, he nibbled on it, rolling the nub with his tongue.

"Yes. Do that." She lowered herself onto his cock, once again flooding him with her heat.

He sucked harder, gripping her breasts so he wouldn't grab her hips and force her down on him.

"That is so good." She began moving faster, finally.

He moved to her other breast, his tongue lavishing her nipple, sucking it into his mouth like a starving babe. She reached for his hair, almost pulling it out by the roots. Unable to stop himself, he ground his hips upwards, driving his cock further into her moist heat.

"Damnit," she gasped, almost collapsing into him.

He held her to him, her heart pounding between her breasts, the vibration pulsating through him. He moved in and out of her again, realizing she held herself above him far enough to ease his ability to move. He smiled against her breast. She had surrendered to him. He drove into her harder, her body jerking against him.

"Explode on me, Trudy." He spoke with her nipple still in his mouth, intentionally teasing it with his teeth. "I want to feel your cum trickle down my balls."

She dropped her head over his, her breath scorching his scalp, turning his brain to mush. She would make him come no matter how hard he fought it. And he wanted her climax, needed to feel her contract around him. Her surrender would mean her compliance, her trust. And he needed that right now more than anything. Without it, he would never be able to protect her.

He didn't expect her to jump off of him. And she moved too fast for him to stop her. Reaching for her, it took a minute for his muddled senses to realize she'd knelt between his legs. Her slender fingers wrapped around the shaft of his cock, using her cum that soaked it as a natural lubricant. She stroked him, moving up and down while she licked her lips.

"You're going to come now." She shot a look at him, torturing him with her calm expression. Never had he seen such beauty wrapped around so much spunk.

Thoughts rattled through his brain. If he came, he wanted to see his white cream dripping off her breasts, or maybe splattered over her mouth. But the way she stroked him, teasing and egging him on at the same time, made it real hard to decide.

All he could do was watch when she lowered her face over him, her blonde hair falling around his dick like a silken cloak. The heat of her mouth consumed him, her moist tongue wrapping around his cock.

"Shit. Darlin', that is so good." Grabbing her hair, he pushed her down on his cock.

Instead of protesting, she sucked him in, her mouth tightening around him, bathing him with moist heat. She began stroking him with her lips, moving up and down while her tongue batted at him.

Pressure built inside him, his muscles hardening. She would suck the life out of him if he didn't stop her. But he had no desire at all to make her quit what she was doing.

"I'm going to come." He gritted his teeth, feeling the hot semen release into her mouth.

She swallowed, her mouth constricting around him. And when she pulled her mouth back from him, he had no strength to hold her in place.

Chapter Fifteen

Trudy fell back on her haunches, the salty taste of his cum lingering in her mouth. His thick cream covered her lower lip and part of her chin. She could feel it. Wiping her mouth with the back of her hand, she stared up at Adam.

"What is it about you?" Everything about him baffled her.

The last thing she had wanted to do was fuck him. Okay. That was a lie. It was the first thing she'd wanted to do. But she'd promised herself that she wouldn't. All Adam Knight had to do was beckon with an outstretched hand and she'd gone to him, her every care thrown to the wind.

Adam looked down at her, an overly content grin on his face. "If you want more, come here." He grabbed his still-hard cock. "I know you haven't come yet."

She wanted to slap him, beat some sense into him, somehow take that smug look off his face. Or at least release the frustrated energy quickly building in her over her own stupidity.

"No. I don't want to come here." She stood up, wiping her face with the back of her hand. "You disappear for a week, without a word, and then prance back into my life like you never left."

Her pussy throbbed, and for some reason getting angry with him made her want to climb right back on to that waiting cock of his and ride out her orgasm. She shoved her desires away, knowing that giving in to him would only allow him to continue to use her like this. And she wouldn't be able to handle him waltzing in and out of her life without notice.

"I missed you, too." He stood, towering over her in the dark kitchen. "But I can't always say when I will leave or when I will return."

Those carnal good looks of his could make her forget her name if she wasn't careful. Focusing on her anger, knowing she was in the right here, she turned away from him. He would seduce her all over again and she wouldn't be any man's whore.

"Like hell you missed me." All she knew about his house was the way back to the front door. She walked in that direction. "The first I see you in a week and you are out running with another bitch."

"And what were you doing out running alone when you know you shouldn't have been?"

She'd needed time alone. Spending every minute with the sensual Margo had taken its toll. Those few moments in her room when Margo had tried to seduce her had left her so worked up her body had been on pins and needles. More than anything she had wanted to see Adam, for him to touch her, and yes…fuck her. And she had hated herself for being so weak.

Seeing him running with another bitch should have proved to her that he had no real feelings for her. He probably knew he would get a piece of tail that night. Since Trudy had run the other woman off, he'd fucked her instead. And she had let him do it.

She waved her hand in the air, brushing off his comment, not sure who she was more disgusted with — him or herself.

"You got what you wanted." She headed for the door. It would be safe to head back to her room by now. And she needed to get out of here.

A powerful hand hit the wooden door just above her head before she could turn the door handle.

"Where in the hell do you think you are going?" His harsh whisper gave her chills.

She ducked out from under him.

Any other time, she would have enjoyed exploring the simple living area, the natural wood furniture, old and comfortable looking. The large fireplace standing empty, giving indication he hadn't been here in a while. More than likely it had the ability to heat most of the open room. She could learn so much about Adam if she took time to explore his home, focus on the details, see who hung in the pictures scattered along the far wall. But learning about his den would only make her want him more. She wasn't stupid. Adam Knight was a womanizer, and somehow she needed to learn to tell him no.

Chasing off any other female he chooses to run with is not the way to tell him no.

"I hardly plan on staying here." She crossed her arms over her breasts, wishing she had some clothes to put on. At least outside she could return to her fur. "If I leave now, maybe your other woman can show up and you can fuck her too."

"I'm sure she will show up here sooner or later." He wasn't going to even try to deny that there were other women.

She had no clue how to handle a man like this. *You are out of your league, girl.*

Her jealousy clung in the air around her, and she knew he could smell it. But still she shrugged, trying her best not to care that he saw other women. Her heart clamped into a painful ball, while a lump formed in her throat. She did care, and she hated herself for letting another man hurt her.

"Then I'll just get out of your hair." Her mouth was dry, making her voice scratchy. But she would be damned if he would see her cry.

He moved away from the door, slowly approaching her with a predator's glint in those penetrating green eyes. She swallowed, hardly able to do so, and focused on the door. There was no way she could move fast enough to get around him without him stopping her.

"Raven will show up here because she is my assistant." He reached for her and she stepped back quickly. But there was nowhere to go. He grabbed her before she could escape, yanking the side of her head, pulling her hair so she was forced to look up at him. "The Bureau assigned her to me a couple of months ago to help with this case. She had caught up with me shortly before you did. I wasn't running with her. She was following me here so we could work."

"Oh." The lump in her throat dissipated as quickly as it had appeared. When his lips pursed into the making of a smile, she worried she might start to cry. "That's not how it appeared."

"I realize that." He pulled her closer, the heat and power coming from his massive frame making it hard for her to think clearly. His fingers tangled further through her hair. She had to let her head fall back to keep his tugging from hurting. "And I realize that you were willing to challenge her for the right to run with me."

Uh-oh. He had to notice that one small detail.

"Animal instinct runs strong. I overreacted." Her excuse sounded lame even to her.

"I don't think so." His other hand moved to the lower part of her back, the heat of his touch melting through her.

She couldn't catch her breath. And every time she inhaled, her breasts brushed against the coarse hair on his chest. He pressed her to him, spreading his fingers over her back. Unable to look away, she did her best to inhale before his mouth descended on hers.

His kiss made her knees go weak. It had to be because she was still aroused from riding him. He parted her lips with his tongue and let her taste his heat, his carnal need for her.

She should be terrified. And maybe she was. Shivers raced through her. This werewolf guided pack leaders, had more power than anyone she had ever known, and would not take no for an answer. But excitement pooled deep inside her, turning to fiery heat while her pussy throbbed, aching for his attention.

He tore his mouth from hers, leaving her struggling to breathe. She realized she hung on him, leaning hard against his solid frame so she wouldn't fall over. As strong as he was, with all the raw power he possessed, he would want a strong lover.

She tried to straighten, stand on her own two feet, but he tightened his grip on her, pinning her to him.

"I think you left your pack searching for something…someone." He trailed moist kisses to her neck. "And you think that someone might be me."

Damn his arrogance. He nibbled on the tender spot just to the side of her collarbone and she thought her insides might turn to Jell-o.

"You are mighty sure of yourself." And it wasn't right that characteristic in him turned her on so much.

"Uh-huh." He gripped her rear end, pressing her against his still hard cock. "You never told me why you were out running by yourself when you shouldn't have been."

"I…uh…" She'd been out looking for him, but she would be damned if he would know that.

"There are humans on a rampage, with inside knowledge on how to locate werewolves." He quit kissing her and gripped her arms.

Instantly she wanted his muscular heat pressing against her again.

"Humans can't catch me."

"Can you outrun a bullet?" His expression grew serious, the darkness in the room shadowing his features. "If they injure you, they can catch you."

Humans had been the last thing on her mind. She'd heard Adam was in town while running around with Margo, talking to pack members. The first chance she had, she'd made an excuse to leave the queen bitch's side, and had taken off looking for him.

"I don't scare that easily." She remembered seeing the humans running through the woods like a pack of fools with their rifles. She'd turned tail and run straight back to

Adam. Well that was because there was power in numbers.

He ran his thumbs up and down her arms, giving her chills although she was hardly cold. If anything, it seemed a bit warm in his house.

"There is a difference between being scared, and being sensible when you detect danger."

He was right and she knew it. But it seemed so submissive to concede to him. She pulled out of his grasp, crossing her arms. His gaze dropped to the swell of her breast, but immediately returned to her face. The man wouldn't be sidetracked.

"If you think for a moment that I am not sensible, then you can forget about touching me ever again." Muscles rippled in his chest. He, too, crossed his arms, his lips pursing as if he weren't accustomed to anyone taking this tone with him. Well he would see she wouldn't roll over for him. "I was very aware of the pending attack by the humans, but..."

She'd almost said that she wanted to be with him. The second John had told her and Margo of the danger, all of her thoughts had gone to Adam. It was more than how he fucked her. But if she told him that, she would open herself up to him. She didn't know if she could allow herself to be that vulnerable yet. This werewolf ran without a pack, lived in exile. He didn't answer to anyone. Would she be able to get him to answer to her?

She stuck her chin out. "But I'd heard there were some members of the pack running outside of town. I'm faster than American werewolves and so went to see if I could find them."

Those damned green eyes burrowed into her. She thought she noticed a muscle twitch just along his jawbone. But she held her ground, not daring to look away. More than anything, she wouldn't let him smell the lie she'd just told.

"I see." His lips barely moved. Nor did any of the other muscles in his body when he moved closer, closing in the space between them. He seemed to grow in size in front of her. "If you ever lie to me again, I will bend you over my knee and spank that adorable ass of yours until it's pink."

Heat rushed through her at the suggestion, her pussy swelling in spite of her efforts to appear put out by his threat.

"You lay a hand on me, Adam Knight, and you will have a fight on your hands." She put her hands on her hips, seeing she needed to put him in his place instead of buckling to his accusations.

Without hesitating, he cupped her breast, those long fingers slowly stroking her skin. "You won't stop me from touching you."

She smacked his hand away, not even thinking, which maybe she should have. One eyebrow rose while his green eyes seemed to glow in the dark. His jaw moved, as if he ground his teeth, or they were growing.

Werewolves are taught not to change in the house at the same age they are potty trained. Allowing the change in someone else's home would be unheard of. But the menacing look on Adam's face let her know she better move quickly, or surrender.

Surrendering was not in her nature.

"I will not be bullied by any werewolf." Memories of Matthew, her deceased mate, coercing her into doing what he wanted flooded through her with a bile taste.

She hadn't given him a thought since she'd arrived in Fargo. The fact that he came to mind now, by Adam trying to manipulate her actions, pissed her off.

"Then do as you're told, and don't lie to me. We'll have no problems."

"You don't own me." She had to stand up to him.

This time when he tried to grab her, she ducked around him. Anger made it real hard to control the change, her emotions egging the carnal side of her to take over. Her bones ached to distraction to alter, shrink and thicken. Hairs prickled along her spine before she could stop them.

Running to the other side of the room, she halted before she fell to all fours, struggling to slow her breathing and her pounding heart. Reversing the change and regaining her wits about her took only a moment. But that one moment of fighting for control allowed Adam to pounce on her.

Strong arms wrapped around her, lifted her, the heat of his body consuming her as rapidly as a forest fire. Before she could react he had her in his arms, crushing her to him. Arousal consumed her anger. Matthew never made her feel like this. She wanted Adam with such a vengeance it took everything she had not to beg him to fuck her silly.

"I never suggested you needed to be owned." He whispered so softly, his voice so soothing, she relaxed, turning into him and running her hand up his chest. "But I will protect you. And you are safer here while I put this ugliness with the humans to rest."

"What's about to happen?" She looked up at him and saw demons tormenting his expression. She doubted he would share everything he knew, but the intent look on his face made her feel he wanted to, needed to unload the burden of knowledge he possessed.

Working to calm down, she realized maybe he needed her compliance to help him handle the work laid out before him. Even though he offered the tough guy exterior, it had to be a challenge to fight to save your own kind. Packs all over relied on Adam to protect them. And he was only one werewolf.

Instead of answering her, he let her slide out of his arms, his hard cock tormenting her when she brushed over it. His chest hair teased her nipples to distraction. It took more than a bit of effort not to continue to slide to her knees and take his cock in her mouth.

One hand went to her rear, clutching her to him, while he tangled his fingers through her hair with his other hand. Then he kissed her. Hard, aggressive, bending her over while he devoured all she would give to him. He held her to him like he would never let go, like he needed her strength to maintain his own.

Neither of them spoke for a moment when the kiss ended. He stared down at her, not moving, staring deep into her gaze, searching for something she didn't know. His rough hand brushed over her back, until he cupped her head, holding her so she wouldn't look away from him.

"I'm going to leave, and you'll stay here until I return."

Chapter Sixteen

Adam had no idea if Trudy would stay at his house or not. Instinct told him more than once to imprison her there, lock her in with everything she needed. But he was driven by more than just instinct. He knew if she didn't want to stay there, nothing he could do would keep her there. Thoughts of telling Raven to stay there with her, serve as a bodyguard, crossed his mind. Raven wouldn't be able to confine Trudy though. He knew that. Nothing could hold his willful female if she didn't want to be held.

That bothered him. It made him sick. It distracted his thoughts.

But he was no pup. Taking care of the human werewolf hunter couldn't wait. And if he had to hunt Trudy down afterward, then so be it.

He'd told her as much, too. The surprised expression she gave him while she stood in his doorway still remained engraved in his memory.

"If you aren't here when I return, I will find you," he had told her. "And if I have to do that, you won't like the mood I'm in once you're found."

The way she had licked her lips, staring up at him, acting like she would speak but then deciding not to, made it clear to him that she understood his meaning. But the spark he'd seen in her eyes and the flush of pink that had traveled over her face told him she liked the idea of him chasing her.

But damnit to hell, this wasn't a game. He prayed she would use her intelligence and see that. He'd told her how to set the security system once he left. And he knew there was enough fresh meat in the house to last at least a week. God help everyone if he had to be gone that long.

Slowing down at the customs booth, he endured the bored customs officer's questions before driving on. At least they hadn't pulled him over to search his car. Not that he had anything to hide, but he wasn't in the mood to deal with any more humans than necessary.

"How long will you be staying?"

It was the same question the custom's officer had asked when he'd entered Canada. He handed his Visa to the motel clerk.

"I'm not sure yet." He didn't want to be here at all. "I'll pay by the day."

The motel clerk nodded, turning to run his Visa through the machine, while Adam looked around the small, unimpressive lobby. A minute later, the clerk handed him his Visa, and the motel key.

"Enjoy your stay in Canada." The clerk smiled, his human scent reminding Adam of the unpleasant reason why he was here.

He had no unpacking to do, and had no desire to get comfortable in the plain room he would be staying in, compliments of the Bureau. Werewolf Affairs knew their agents seldom slept in the motel rooms assigned to them while in the field. He doubted the budget covering travel expenses would ever allow him to stay somewhere en vogue.

Needing to kill time before dark, he stretched out on the bed then punched the auto dial button on his phone to his house. It rang twice before Trudy picked up.

"Hello, Knight residence." Her tone was soft, husky, like she'd been sleeping.

"Hello, sweetheart."

There was a brief pause and he wondered what she was doing.

"Adam? Where are you?" Maybe he had woken her; she sounded clearer now.

"In a motel room. What are you doing?"

"Not a damned thing." Her tone turned pouty, his cock stirring in his pants at her breathy tone. "I was asleep."

"In my bed?" He pictured her curled under his covers, her blonde hair spread over his pillow.

"Yes, in your bed. Would you have me sleep on the couch?"

"Never. What are you wearing?"

Her low chuckle worked like fire through his bloodstream.

"I'm naked." She made a cooing sound through the phone and he imagined her stretching, blankets tangling around her.

His cock began throbbing.

"Were you dreaming of me?" He sure was fantasizing about her.

"You wish, wolf man." Her chuckle gave him chills, which did nothing to soothe the heat surging through him. "Actually you woke me from a dream of chasing a Cariboo."

His adorable *lunewulf* bitch dreamed of freedom. Well he didn't like being confined either, but this was a matter of protecting her life. He hoped she saw that.

"Margo called me earlier," she added.

"What did she want?" He guessed she either was looking for him, itching for two men to fuck her again, or she wanted Trudy.

"I guess to make sure I was okay." Her voice faded. There was more. "Or maybe she wanted you."

"She was checking on you." He sensed her jealousy, but had nothing to answer for.

"Adam?"

He knew what she was going to ask by the way she said his name.

"Yes?"

"Have you fucked Margo?" She whispered the question. He knew she feared the answer, but curiosity had gotten the better of her.

Well he wouldn't lie. "Yes."

"Oh."

The swinging lifestyle was very strange to people who knew nothing about it. He would give her time to digest that knowledge. She would likely hound him with more questions later.

"She's tried to…uhh…seduce me, too."

Thoughts of Trudy and Margo naked, intertwined, hands roaming over each other's sensual bodies, about made him come. He grabbed his cock through his jeans, taking a moment to breathe.

Forcing himself to stand, he walked into the small bathroom.

"Did you like it?" He wondered if Trudy had been with women before. Her hesitancy made him think she hadn't.

"It made me think of you," she whispered.

The coldest of waterfalls wouldn't save him now. Quickly undoing his jeans, he let them fall to the floor then padded back to the bed. He wanted details on Trudy's encounter.

"Yeah?" He stretched out, resuming his position of lying down, and grabbed his throbbing cock. Blood rushed through him so fast he could hear it pounding in his ears. "And what did the two of you do?"

She sighed, and he swore he felt her breath caress him. A mental picture of her fingering herself while she talked to him sent heat rushing through him.

"We kissed. Or I should say, she kissed me."

"You didn't kiss her back?"

"Well yeah. I did." She paused, her breathing heavy. He ached to know what she was doing. "And…well…she touched me. I'd never thought about being with a woman before," she added quickly.

"Do you want to be with her now?"

She didn't answer right away. He would give her time to consider. Never would he press her to do something she didn't want to do. Fantasizing was one thing, but they were talking about the real thing here.

"I want you." Her confession rippled through him so fast he couldn't stop the moisture that trickled over his fingers from his cock.

"I want you too, sweetheart. Real bad." More than anything he wanted to bury his cock deep inside her heat.

He bet that pussy of hers was on fire right about now. He squeezed his eyes shut, needing all of his strength to control his actions.

"When will you be home?"

He liked the way that sounded. His woman waited for him at his home.

"Not soon enough," he admitted honestly, wishing he could give her a better answer.

Someone knocked on the door, and he jumped in spite of himself, gripping his cock painfully.

"Just a minute," he called out.

"What is it?" Trudy sounded louder, obviously alerted to the change in the mood.

"Someone is at the door, sweetheart. I'll call you back as soon as I can."

She mumbled something when he told her goodbye, and reluctantly he hung up the phone, once again putting a country's border between them.

Struggling into his jeans, he then opened the motel room door so Raven could enter. She moved past him to the round table next to the curtains, and plopped down her briefcase, which he knew housed her laptop.

"Are you ready?" she asked instead of saying hello.

"Just waiting for it to get dark." He turned from her, heading to the bathroom, deciding to shower and fantasize about Trudy, while his assistant set up shop.

By the time it was dark, his mood had turned foul. He paced behind Raven, who sat facing her computer at the table. Trudy hadn't sounded too pleased to hang up the phone so abruptly. Thoughts of her naked on his bed, fingering that sweet cunt of hers, or intertwined with Margo, still plagued his system.

"I have an exact location for you." Raven slid her chair to the side, pointing to her monitor.

He moved closer, studying the map she'd brought up on the screen. "I can find it."

The sooner he put an end to this human's madness, the better.

The chilly night air helped soothe his irritated senses a little. Staying focused was imperative. From what he knew of this human, this Christopher Hordan, he would need to be alert, and prepared for anything. The man had successfully located many packs in the northwest part of the United States and killed many werewolves. Not an easy feat for a human.

A northern wind bit through his skin when he shed his clothes. Shivering while allowing the change to tear through him made adrenaline pump even faster through his system. Bones popped, contorting, a pain so exquisite he shut his eyes briefly, allowing the beast within him to take over. Fur spread over him, replacing the fragile human skin that couldn't keep him warm. His body temperature soared, clearing his head when the frigid night air no longer distracted him.

Blackness around him faded, his vision changing and nighttime no longer blinding him. Smells of the earth, the trees, and fading scents of the nightlife filled his nostrils. Arching his back, he flexed the muscles that had grown and changed into that of a werewolf. He was ready to go meet Christopher Hordan.

Come and get me, motherfucker.

No human would get the better of him. Werewolves were the complete species, given what humans lacked. And he wouldn't allow this half of a whole to bring down his kind.

Relying on memory to guide him, picturing the map in his head that Raven had shown him on the computer, he tore across countryside. Christopher Hordan didn't live in town. But then he couldn't. The paranoia of his own kind wouldn't allow him to indulge in the killing of werewolves. If, in his warped way of thinking, he somehow thought he did his kind a favor, Hordan's own would kill him for consorting with monsters. Humans were strange. He accepted their ways, but never claimed to understand them.

Spruce trees grew thick around him, their sweet earthy scent invigorating. Adam slowed his gait, entering into the thickness of the forest. He was getting closer. Taking a minute to absorb his surroundings and not let the smell of the spruce distract him, he searched the forest, narrowing his eyes while noting all that was around him.

Little to no wildlife moved around him. Either another predator had passed by recently, although he didn't smell the trail of one, or they had heard him coming, and took to hiding.

He perked his ears, stopping so that he could listen. The night chill in the air barely penetrated his coat, and felt good after running for so long. But he didn't stop to enjoy the cold night. Something wasn't right. It was too quiet.

Moving slowly, making no sound for a werewolf his size, he realized he was probably quite close to Hordan's home.

You even scare away the wildlife.

A sharp pain ripped through his thigh. He turned, barely having time to acknowledge the wound, before he fell, blackness engulfing him.

Chapter Seventeen

It took a minute for Trudy to remember where she was when she awoke the next morning. Glancing at the digital clock on the table next to the bed, she noticed the cordless phone where she'd left it the night before after talking to Adam.

The ache, the longing for him she'd bared the night before returned with a vengeance. She tossed off the covers, the room suddenly too warm. Lying naked on Adam's bed didn't help matters much either.

"Shit," she grumbled. Her pussy throbbed, desire filling a bedroom that seemed empty to her. The whole damned house seemed empty, a shell, lacking life and happiness.

She shouldn't be letting herself get so worked up over this werewolf. What had happened to wanting her independence?

An emptiness consumed her, pulling her stomach into a knot. There was no way she could sit idly all day in this house, wondering what Adam was doing, who he was with, if he was safe.

But this is what he does — he roams and protects.

Could she live with a werewolf who danced with danger on a daily basis?

Showering didn't help her mood. Nothing in the kitchen looked good to eat. And she had no clothes here. Remaining naked all day would simply make her crave

Adam more. Wandering around his home in one of his shirts didn't bother her, but it would be nice to have a few of her things here.

If you leave here, I will hunt you down.

She smiled while staring out his front living room window, the open view of the Badlands calling her to run and play. Imagining Adam stalking her, hunting her down, sent shivers through her. He would be a ruthless hunter, she was sure of it. And even with her speed, she had a feeling he would be able to catch her.

And what if she left? He didn't own her. Obviously the world wasn't too dangerous for him to be out gallivanting around. She'd managed for thirty years to take care of herself. She sure could do it now. Besides, leaving his home didn't mean she didn't want to spend time with him. He wasn't here and there was no reason for her to be idle while he was gone.

Thoughts of their phone call being interrupted the night before haunted her. Someone had knocked on his motel room door, and she just knew who that someone was. That chubby little assistant of his, taking advantage of her not being there.

Now you're being ridiculous.

She gave herself a shake, working to shrug out of the jealousy that she could smell filling the room. Maybe a run would be a good idea, just to clear the cobwebs. She could stay in the area, be back here in an hour or so. Out here in the middle of nowhere running during the day wouldn't be a problem.

A car pulled off the two-lane highway and headed down the long narrow drive toward the house. Trudy's heart pounded in her chest while she backed away from the open window. Adam hadn't suggested there might be company. And all she had on was one of his flannel shirts. Quickly she made sure all of the buttons on it were buttoned, wondering who in the hell would be driving all the way out here. If they came this far, they were here to see Adam.

She smiled, sighing with relief, when she recognized the Honda Accord at the same time that Margo jumped out of the driver's side.

"I'm here to rescue you." Margo grinned when Trudy opened the front door. "You will die of boredom out here waiting for that werewolf to return."

"I was getting a bit restless." She suddenly felt guilty about leaving. "Adam was real adamant about my staying here though."

Margo waved her hand in a dismissive gesture. "I'm sure he was. They would have all of us chained to the bed if they thought they could get away with it."

Heat flushed through her when Margo let her gaze drop, taking in Trudy's attire. She didn't know why the quick explanation came out of her mouth. "I came here in my fur."

"He wants you confined to his home, and naked. Sounds kinky." Margo's laughter made it clear she approved. "Come on. We'll say we're getting you some of your things."

"John doesn't know you are here?" She followed Margo out the door, and then turned to set the house alarm.

"Well he knows I am rounding up some of our rural pack members." She'd rounded the car by the time Trudy reached it, and winked over the hood. "And if memory serves, John views you as a member of our pack."

Trudy wanted to know how Margo knew where Adam lived, but wasn't sure she wanted to hear the answer. She didn't say much during their drive back to Fargo, letting Margo chat on about pack business. Several times her cell phone rang, and then Trudy stared out the window while Margo reassured a pack member that all was fine.

"There have just been a few disturbances. John wants us to keep a low profile for the time being."

She had to admit, Margo was good. With a sickening feeling in her stomach she accepted the fact that Margo was probably good at everything. She refused to allow an image of Adam fucking Margo surface in her brain, instead turning when Margo said something.

"Thinking about him?" Margo asked, dropping her cell phone between them.

"Yeah." It wasn't a lie.

"I told you before. He hasn't had any women around since he came to Fargo." She reached for Trudy, taking her hand and squeezing it. "I wouldn't be surprised if he was thinking about you right now, too."

Margo's touch was warm, soft, her words reassuring. Trudy licked her lips, wondering what it would be like to love one werewolf, but have sex with another werewolf.

You had three mates and fucked all of them. But this was different. There hadn't been any other women involved. At least none that joined them for sex when she was around.

"I'm not sure what to think about him. Or what he thinks."

Margo didn't answer, but pulled her hand away, leaving Trudy's skin tingling where she'd touched her. They entered Fargo, and Margo drove straight to where Trudy had a room, and everything she owned was.

"I can see why he wanted to keep you naked." Margo walked behind Trudy when they were alone in her room. She ran her fingers up her back, immediately making Trudy's nipples harden from the touch.

Trudy cupped her own breasts, wanting to cover her aroused nipples, and play with them at the same time.

"Margo," she whispered. "This isn't right."

Margo turned her around, and Trudy immediately noticed her intense expression. Everything about Margo showed how turned on she was. Her caramel skin glowed with a sensual flush. Margo ran her tongue over her full lips, giving them a glossy hue.

"You don't want me to," Margo guessed, although she didn't take her hands off of Trudy's shoulders.

"No. Well. I don't know." She didn't know what to think at the moment. "We are all alone."

Margo laughed, pulling Trudy to her and hugging her.

"John doesn't mind." She let Trudy go and moved to the bed, sitting on the edge of it. "He loves hearing all of the details. But I agree. If he were here we could fuck him after playing with each other."

She remembered telling Adam about her last encounter with Margo. She had lain in his bed, fingering her pussy, listening to his breathing grow raspy over the phone while she shared the details of how Margo had almost seduced her.

But what would Adam say if she told him she had fucked John? Would that turn him on, too? She couldn't imagine that it would. More like piss him off.

Her fingers shook when she pulled her shirt over her head. "I guess all of this is new to me."

"You had three mates but you've never been with a woman?"

Margo's question surprised her. She pulled her jeans on, fidgeting with the buttons with shaking fingers.

"I didn't ask to have three mates; it was the law of our pack." She didn't see any reason to go into the atrocities of her past. "But no. I've never been with another woman."

"To have three werewolves who you could fuck anytime you wanted. I love doing more than one werewolf at a time."

Her words bit at Trudy, and she looked at Margo in time to see her nibble at her lower lip, a faraway look in her eyes. John didn't mind sharing his mate with another werewolf. And apparently Margo wouldn't mind sharing John with her.

Did Margo seduce Adam into joining them for a romp in their bed?

She wouldn't let Margo smell her jealousy. Sighing, she gathered her few possessions together. "I guess I'm ready."

Margo looked up at her quickly, as if being pulled from her thoughts.

"Okay. I'll take you over to the house for now." She stood, looking for a minute like she was trying to decide something. Her soft brown eyes searched the room briefly before her expression relaxed.

"I hope I haven't offended you." Trudy didn't know why she was apologizing. Shy of being queen bitch, Margo had no right over her. If she didn't want a bisexual encounter, she didn't need to give her reasons why. Still, something in Margo's expression made her press the issue. "When I'm around you...when you touch me...it makes me think of Adam."

"If it bothers you, maybe you should talk to Adam." Margo spoke softly, like a mother soothing her cub.

"No. I'm not worried about his feelings on the matter." She focused on her toes, drawing an imaginary line on the floor. She was muddling this whole matter, when the truth was plain and simple. She took a deep breath, unable to look up, or she would lose her nerve. "It's my feelings. I think I'm bothered by the fact that you have fucked him."

"Oh."

The silence that followed lingered so heavily in the room, Trudy could hardly stand it. Finally she looked up, knowing from the heat on her cheeks that she was blushing furiously. Margo had her lips pursed together, her mouth making a perfect heart shape. But her eyes had that faraway look in them again.

"I've never fucked Adam when John wasn't there. Nor would I want to." She almost sounded hurt.

Just great. Now Trudy had offended her. She hadn't expected to suddenly feel the role of the defensive.

Margo stood, straightening her clothes with a gentle brush of her hands. Always the graceful one, she led the way out of the room, without saying anything else.

"I want you to know something." Margo turned to her after starting the car. "Now that he is with you, I wouldn't fuck him without your consent. I respect that he is your werewolf, and if you'll remember, I gave you my blessing."

"I never said he was my werewolf," she mumbled.

Margo laughed, pulling away from the curb and heading toward her home. "Well he might as well be. Because I tell you, darling, he has made it quite clear that you belong to him. You may as well admit to claiming him in return."

Trudy ran her fingers through her hair, suddenly very confused.

Within minutes they were at Margo's, the extra cars parked in the drive drawing both women's attention.

"You've got company." Trudy stated the obvious, glancing over to catch Margo's concerned expression. Her brows narrowed as she looked from one parked car to the next.

"It doesn't look good," was all she said.

Trudy followed Margo after they parked on the street in front of the house. Tension weighed heavy in the living room, several men glancing in their direction. Two older werewolves, frustration lingering around them, nodded while Margo closed the front door behind Trudy.

"What we need to know is what will happen after Knight kills this werewolf hunter." A third werewolf, younger than the rest, had his back to the ladies when he spoke to John Campbell.

"I was worried about you." John moved around the man, wrapping his arm around Margo, while smiling over her head at Trudy. He turned his attention to the younger werewolf who had just spoken. "And that is the plan we are working on right now."

Trudy glanced around the room. The two older werewolves, old enough to be her father, if he were still alive, looked grim. The younger werewolf, carrot-top red hair looking a bit too ruffled, appeared more animated. He ignored the women, too wound up into the conversation.

"We need to do something about these humans on a rampage. Knight may be able to kill their leader, but he can't be everywhere at once." The young redhead walked around John so that he faced him.

John gave Margo a squeeze, whispering something in her ear. Margo let go of him and took Trudy by the hand, guiding her toward the kitchen. Trudy wanted to hear what they were saying about Adam. He hadn't told her he was headed out to kill a human. She wanted to know every detail about what he was doing. Her stomach curled into an uncomfortable knot. He wasn't in any danger, was he?

"John is hungry." Margo let go of Trudy's hand once they were alone in the kitchen. "Come to think of it, so am I. Want to help me put lunch together?"

She wasn't sure she could eat anything. Spending time with Margo had unsettled her, but now thoughts of Adam plagued her, too. She wanted to be with him, not here with a pack she barely knew.

Margo pulled cold cuts out of the refrigerator, and pointed to one of the counters. "We might as well make enough sandwiches for everyone. Will you get the plates?"

She busied herself doing as Margo asked, while she wondered what Adam was doing now. Where was this human? And why was he a werewolf killer? Try as she would to get answers from the men's conversation in the other room, nothing they said helped.

"Are you okay?" Margo asked while dumping potato salad into a serving bowl to put on the table. One thing that seemed to stay the same no matter what pack she visited, the queen bitch was always the skilled hostess.

Trudy watched her mound the yellow mush into the ornate bowl. "I can't help wondering where Adam is, and if he's okay."

Margo met her gaze, her expression serious. "You have fallen for a wandering werewolf."

She left the kitchen, carrying the potato salad to the dining room table. "Grab the meat." She gestured with a nod to the plate of cold cuts she'd prepared and Trudy helped put the food on the table.

"I would just like to know where he is," Trudy confessed a few minutes later after the men started to linger around the dining room table.

She'd followed Margo back into the kitchen, knowing she wouldn't be able to eat a bite of food. Margo turned to her, understanding in her smile.

"I hate to see you worrying." She caressed Trudy's face, a light touch with her fingertips over her cheek.

Trudy looked down, not wanting to be consoled, but informed. Margo must have sensed her frustration. She ran her fingers through Trudy's hair, her grip soft, but enough to make Trudy look at her. The gesture was possessive, controlling, just the way Adam would have touched her. Her insides flip-flopped, although she knew it wasn't because Margo's touch turned her on. The only reason she reacted to the intimate caress was because she was thinking of Adam.

"Probably the one werewolf who knows where he is would be his assistant, Raven." Margo stroked the side of Trudy's head, another intimate caress that sent tingles down Trudy's spine.

She ignored the sensation Margo's touch gave her. Distracting thoughts of Adam's assistant, and the knock on his motel room door ending their conversation the night before made it hard to concentrate.

She wouldn't be jealous. If the werewolf wanted his assistant, then she would simply back off and continue on with her life. But she would find out where this human werewolf killer lived. She would know where Adam was, and what he was doing.

Chapter Eighteen

Adam blinked once, then twice, trying to clear his vision. It was still dark. He sat up, the ground beneath him hard and cold. The air smelled stale and dampness clung to him. Where in the hell was he?

He remembered getting shot and a net of some type covering him. But that was it. The more he thought about what might have happened, the more his head began to throb. And that wasn't all that hurt. He ran his hands over his body, realizing quickly enough that he wasn't injured, just sore and naked.

Whoever had captured him must have used a tranquilizer gun. A strong tranquilizer. One intended to take out a werewolf. They had chained him to the wall as a werewolf. Apparently he'd changed to his human form while knocked out.

Well, he had set out to find Christopher Hordan, and it appeared he'd found him. The human werewolf killer had captured him. He would bet money on it. Except that he didn't have any money, or clothes.

Running his hands over the metal collar that was clasped around his neck, he fingered the chain attached to it. The chain wasn't more than two feet long, not long enough to allow him to stand. And it appeared to be linked to a stone wall.

A banging sounded and his body tensed. Sore muscles made their presence known throughout his body. He didn't doubt he'd been dragged through the forest once knocked out. That and sleeping on the hard floor would explain why he ached.

He stretched his legs, finding he could do so easily enough. His prison allowed him that much space. A feeling of claustrophobia washed over him anyway. He didn't like being confined, never had. The fact that he couldn't even stand made it worse.

"Hey!" he yelled at the muffled voices outside. "Remember me?"

He closed his eyes, knowing when that door opened the brightness would blind him anyway. Focusing on the sounds and smells around him, he listened for approaching footsteps.

Silence followed for only a moment. He heard the leaves on the ground crunch outside, small steps, close together. Other footsteps sounded. Someone said something, quietly, possibly under their breath. And then he heard the clink of a key being inserted in a keyhole.

Light flooded the room, its warmth spreading over him. He kept his eyes shut only for a moment, then squinted, allowing them to adjust slowly from the darkness. Dust molecules floated around him, the brightness allowing him to see the stone and mortar prison he'd been confined in. A small square room, no taller than it was wide, hooks on the wall made to hold its prisoners. A werewolf cage.

"So you're awake." A woman spoke, and at the same time the cold end of a rifle prodded his shoulder. "Don't move a muscle, werewolf."

He obliged while someone else reached around him and messed with the chain, releasing it from the wall.

Apparently the collar around his neck was meant to stay. He wondered how much they actually knew about his kind. Changing slightly would give him enough strength to rip the metal off of him.

He eased to his feet, but the room and the door were smaller than he was. Hunching over, he stepped outside glancing around into what appeared to be a backyard surrounded by spruce that offered a severe degree of privacy. Their rich scent wrapped around him, cleansing him from his dark prison.

"This way, werewolf." The human male tugged on his chain, the metal collar rubbing his skin to the point of irritation.

He glared at the human, getting a perverse pleasure out of watching the man sidestep around him, keeping a tight grip on the chain. The human, a man about his size but with no muscle tone to speak of, glanced at the woman carrying the gun.

Adam allowed them to lead him toward the house, deciding disarming the woman at this point would be futile. He'd come here to speak with Christopher Hordan and he hoped that was who they were taking him to.

The second they opened the door to the house, Adam fought to keep his expression calm. The smell of humans made his stomach twist though, and it growled furiously.

"Cooperate and maybe we'll feed you." There was amusement in the woman's voice.

He hadn't eaten in a while, but food hadn't crossed his mind. Glancing at her, he decided her kind might think her pretty. She was athletic-looking, her reddish-blonde hair cropped short, and eyes that looked away from him the second he gave her his attention. But she kept that gun pointed right at him. He guessed it was loaded with another hard tranquilizer.

"Do you have what I like to eat?" he whispered.

Curiosity and fear swarmed around her, her expression showing neither when she looked up at him. She had a hard time focusing on his face, and not letting her gaze drift down his nude body. "If we don't, I guess you'll starve." She sounded harsh, but her feelings spoke otherwise. She wondered about him, the smell around her was too strong.

The smell of another human, covered by a strong aftershave, grabbed his attention. He looked away from the woman, searching for the third human.

"In here." The coward yanking on his chain nodded toward the living room, while leading Adam that way.

With a quick glance, he took in the large room that showed all the signs of a big game hunter. A buck's head with antlers that spread an arm's length hung over the sunken fireplace. A white bass, with its mouth opened wide, gasping for its last breath, hung on the opposite wall. Displays of a human proud of his kill, but hunting to do just that, for sport instead of food.

Two men stood in the living room, big men, who glared at him. One was human with beady eyes that looked pinched under thick black eyelashes. But he noticed immediately that the other didn't smell human, not completely. A trace of werewolf lingered around him. But just lingered. He scowled at Adam with dark eyes that looked almost black under waves of dark hair.

"What are you?" he couldn't help but ask.

The man straightened, his frown increasing. This one was a lot younger than the rest and lacked the skill of controlling his emotions, or his temper. For a second Adam thought he would hit him.

"Bring him in here. This isn't a social hour." The loud bark from the other room made everyone in the room grow tense. Either they feared their leader, or they didn't like him.

The coward tugged on Adam's chain, leading him past the two men into the room they apparently guarded.

Adam stopped when he reached the middle of the room, aware of the woman next to him holding the rifle, her emotions clouding him. Her nerves, fear, and curiosity saturated the air. He would bet his nudity distracted her, which made it easier for him to stand naked among them. His body was his only weapon.

"Dear God." A tall man looked at him from behind a desk, removing wire-framed glasses to gawk at him. "Are we barbarians? Find something to put on this werewolf."

He sensed his two escorts glance at each other, more than likely wondering which one should leave his side. The two guards behind him made no sound, but he smelled their aggravation. With all of the humans surrounding him, the odd scent he detected when they were in the living room wasn't as strong. But he smelled werewolf, not strong enough to be full-blooded. He'd always thought stories of half-human, half-werewolf were myths.

"Mary!" The man pointed a finger at the woman with the rifle. "Do you get some cheap thrill out of standing next to this naked beast?"

Mary snorted, or possibly gasped. Adam didn't take his eyes off the man behind the desk while she turned and left the room, shutting the door behind her.

"Are all human women attracted to you?" The man sat in his heavily stuffed leather seat, reclining easily. He removed his glasses, studying Adam.

"I've never noticed." Adam stared at the human in front of him, wishing they were alone so he could detect his scent better.

He guessed the human's age at no more than a couple years older than him. Strawberry blond hair cut short, and slight indentions on either side of the man's face from glasses, gave him a scholarly look. He had a clear complexion, and pale green eyes that offered no secrets. This human wasn't a warrior; his size would be no match in battling a werewolf. Not the look Adam had imagined for Christopher Hordan.

The human tapped his glasses on the desk before unfolding them and carefully putting them on. He looked at Adam over the rims, his expression disbelieving. "I assume you know who I am."

Adam blinked, wanting to move closer so that he could single out the man's scent, but all too aware of the metal collar around his neck. "I have no idea," he muttered, not caring if the human believed him or not. Any show this human offered would only benefit him in knowing his abilities.

The man scoffed. "I'm Christopher Hordan, which you already know. And you are Adam Knight, special agent with Werewolf Affairs."

Impressive. The human had done his homework. His knowledge of Werewolf Affairs bothered Adam, but hopefully Hordan's arrogance would allow him to tell Adam how he knew of such a covert agency.

"The pleasure is all mine," Adam muttered, suddenly aware of growing fear in the human men around him.

Hordan straightened, never taking his gaze from Adam's face. "I doubt any of this is that pleasurable for you."

The door opened behind him, the female's scent filling his nostrils before she appeared. He looked down at her, noticing her glance at his cock before she could stop herself. Quickly she handed him a pair of sweatpants and a sweatshirt then backed away, almost backing into one of the other humans.

"Thank you." He made his voice a little deeper than necessary, a luring tone he'd used on women in the past.

Images of Trudy popped into his head and he found himself comparing the two women. Mary lacked Trudy's strength, her drive. And Mary was scared. Either she didn't want to be here, or she didn't trust the others around her. He couldn't tell just by the emotions he smelled on her. And her facial expression remained relaxed, in spite of the nervous look she gave him before turning to avoid the other human.

Unfolding the drawstring pants, he felt the tug on the chain around his neck when he bent over slightly to put them on. They fit around the waist, but barely made it to his ankles. He didn't care—clothes were clothes. One look at the sweatshirt and he knew it wouldn't fit. He tossed it onto the chair facing Hordan's desk, returning his attention to the werewolf killer.

"Shackle him, Matthew." Hordan looked at the human holding Adam's chain. "And then leave us, all of you."

"But Father…" Mary began to protest.

Adam felt something cold wrap around one wrist, and then his hands were tugged behind his back to be locked together. The chain snaked down his spine, being connected to the handcuffs. He gave the restraints little attention.

Father? Now this is interesting.

He glanced from Mary to Hordan.

"Keep murder in the family, do you?" he taunted, curious how far he could push Hordan. Knowing the man's breaking point would allow him to know when he could overcome the human.

Everyone seemed to still, except Hordan. He moved around his desk faster than Adam guessed him capable. Not stopping until he was inches from Adam's face, the human glared at him, hatred swarming in his dark green eyes.

"Removing werewolves is hardly murder. You are a mutated mistake, the devil's seed, a gross atrocity," he spit into Adam's face. "How dare you attempt to call my actions murder."

A fire burned behind the angry expression on Hordan's face. Adam wondered if the human's green eyes weren't just a bit darker than they had been a moment before. But what really caught his attention was the human's scent. It wasn't right. Christopher Hordan was halfwerewolf, too.

Chapter Nineteen

The rise and fall of the voices downstairs didn't help Trudy's nerves. She paced Margo and John's bedroom where Margo had assured her it would be okay to watch television. But she couldn't concentrate on any show. Clicking the remote, changing channels every few minutes, she strolled from one end of the room to the other, glancing out the window, and then out the bedroom door.

The only place to sit in the bedroom was on their bed, but every time she glanced at the king-sized bed, with its iron floorboard and headboard, her mind conjured up all kinds of possible activity that might have taken place there.

Adam probably fucked Margo on that bed. Every time she imagined him pounding his cock into Margo, a tingling raced through her. She licked her lips, picturing Margo's naked body, the round curve of her rear end, and Adam's cock diving deep inside her. And John would have been there, too. Possibly kneeling in front of Margo, while she sucked his shaft deep into her mouth.

Trudy knew what it was like to be with more than one werewolf. But to seek it out, to enjoy it, crave it. She'd seen the look in Margo's eyes when she had admitted to fucking Adam, how her expression had flushed. Adam was an awesome lover. Any woman would enjoy him.

And that was what Margo had done. She had enjoyed him. She hadn't fallen in love with him. She had John.

She'd told Trudy she wouldn't fuck Adam if John wasn't there. And she'd made it clear that she enjoyed more than one werewolf at a time sexually. It was playing to Margo, nothing more.

So you have nothing to be jealous over. She walked up to the bed, running her finger over the heavy comforter that fell over either side.

"I would love to know what you are thinking right now." Margo's comment startled her.

"Oh. Shit." Trudy's hand went to her heart, unable to stop the ferocious beating that she could feel through her shirt. "I guess I was lost in thought," she stammered, suddenly embarrassed that she hadn't noticed Margo come into the room.

"John wanted me to let you know everyone is gone. You can join us downstairs if you like." Margo moved around the bed, silent in her bare feet. She grinned. "Or I guess we could all watch TV up here."

Margo's suggestive tone left Trudy's mouth dry. Turning away from her, she walked to the window. The cool pane felt good against her hand, and she wanted to press her face against it, needing the coldness to ease the fever that seemed to be racing through her.

"Have you ever had another lady join you two in bed? Or just other men?" She had no idea why she blurted out the question, or even where it came from. She didn't care about their sex life. And the answer didn't matter to her, did it?

"Other couples have joined us a few times, and Adam has several times. That's it." Margo hadn't moved closer. Her voice was calm, her answer quick and to the point.

Trudy sighed. She sensed Margo wanted her to understand, to accept their ways. She turned around, keeping her hands behind her, her fingers resting against the windowpane, its coolness her life thread at the moment.

She studied the beautiful black woman sitting relaxed on her bed. Margo didn't say anything, possibly giving her time to digest what she'd just told her. Trudy licked her lips, wishing for a drink, anything to soothe her dry mouth.

"I've always thought of myself as pretty open-minded. Even when our pack issued the law giving us three mates, I embraced it, excited and willing to mate with all of them."

Margo nodded. "Maybe this is different because of Adam. Did you truly love any of your mates who were assigned to you?"

She had wanted to love them. She'd tried with everything she had to love Matthew. Thoughts of him gave her chills, a cold sweat breaking out over her flushed skin.

"I tried to care about them, but no, I didn't love them. Not the way you love John."

"Or the way you love Adam," Margo added.

Adam. She wanted to find him, needed to know he was okay. But she had a feeling John wouldn't approve of her running alone back to his home, or worse yet out on her own to track him. And she wasn't sure she could stay here in their home with them.

Trudy looked away from the compassionate expression Margo offered her, focusing instead on the lacy curtains bordering the other window in the room.

"I'm not sure what my feelings are for him," she admitted. And it was the truth. She lusted after him. She wouldn't deny that. Her body craved having him buried inside her again. But that wasn't love.

She worried about him. This job he had was a dangerous one. And in spite of his cocky, arrogant manner, he wasn't invincible, even if he was just battling humans.

Margo stood and even barefoot, she hovered over Trudy by a few inches. Her black hair shone from the overhead light, while her brown eyes looked soft, gentle, against her smooth caramel skin. Trudy could see her hardened nipples through Margo's loose fitting T-shirt, but wouldn't speculate if she were aroused or cold.

"But you have feelings. We know you are worried about him." Margo reached up, taking a strand of Trudy's hair and rubbing it between her fingers.

Trudy had the strangest sensation of leaning into Margo's hand. Her actions seemed so motherly. But Trudy had never had a mother. Her grandmother had raised her. And Grandmother Rousseau hadn't taught her to rely on the strength of a mother.

"Of course I am worried about him. He is seeking out a killer." She straightened, relying on her own strength. "But I'm sure he wouldn't have been sent to protect so many packs if he wasn't good at what he does."

"He's the best at what he does," Margo whispered, her fingers running through Trudy's hair, combing it, stroking it. "And he deserves the best. I think he might have found that in you."

Trudy felt her stomach flip-flop, Margo's praise humbling her and exciting her at the same time. She'd

145

never been attracted to a woman before, although she knew a beautiful lady when she saw one. But something raced through her, a curiosity of sorts. What would it be like to make love to a woman?

She took Margo's hand, giving it a friendly squeeze. "You flatter me." She would keep her wits about her, and not be seduced just because her emotions were on a seesaw at the moment.

Margo pulled her into a hug before Trudy had time to react. "I know you want to go back to his place," she whispered in Trudy's ear.

"Am I interrupting something?" John's baritone about made Trudy jump out of her skin.

"Well hell." Margo seemed to have jumped a bit too. She must not have heard her mate approaching either. The floorboards in this house were as solid as a rock.

John chuckled, not seeming a bit bothered that he had startled both of them. "I wondered what you two were up to."

"We were just talking." Margo ran her hand over Trudy's hair and she watched John watch the act.

His fingers flexed into a fist than relaxed. A small sign of the control he must be administering. Of course he had no idea what they'd been doing up here alone. Knowing how his mate was, his imagination could only torture him.

"Margo reassured me that Adam is the best at what he does, and there is nothing to worry about." Somehow having Adam in the conversation made her feel better.

"He will be able to handle the matter," John said with calm resolve. Almost as if he believed everything had already been taken care of.

She would love to know that he was coming home, mission accomplished. Her insides flip-flopped when she remembered his parting words to her. Her pussy throbbed thinking about him hunting her down. But it wouldn't be a game. And she didn't want to imagine what Adam would be like angry. Somehow she needed to get out of here.

"I believe you." Her calm exterior impressed even her. Inside, her stomach was forming a painful knot, while her heart refused to slow to its normal beat. She needed a long cool drink, and a place to nap—alone—for a while. "Maybe we'll hear from him tomorrow. Should I just take the spare bedroom tonight?"

"I stripped the sheets from it this morning." Margo moved toward the bedroom door. "I can get fresh sheets."

John reached for her, stopping her. "You two sleep in here. I'll take the couch."

He kissed Margo's forehead, and then smiled at Trudy before retreating. The overwhelming sensation of suddenly being caged in consumed her. He would ensure neither of them left the house, leaving them together in an upstairs room, with him asleep at the bottom of the stairs.

"That was nice of him." Trudy didn't know what else to say, awkwardness washing over her. And she hated the feeling. She shouldn't feel uneasy about anything, other than how Adam would react when he came home and she wasn't there.

"He thinks you are going to try to sneak out and return to Adam's." Margo winked at her, reading her thoughts.

Margo offered her an oversized shirt to sleep in, and then changed into her own pajamas.

"I've only worn these a few times," she mused, looking down at the baggy shirt and matching pajama bottoms she had on. "They're comfy."

"They look it." Trudy edged toward the bed, not sure which side she should take.

Margo slid under the covers on the opposite side, so Trudy followed suit. Laying there in the dark, she wondered if sleep would ever come to her.

"Good night," Margo whispered, rolling over so her back was to Trudy. "Sleep well."

Trudy doubted she would. And that annoyed her. Adam seemed to have control over her and she didn't even know where he was. With a sigh, she knew she couldn't give him that much power. He wouldn't want a wimpy werewolf. Even if he thought he wanted her to obey his every word. She needed to think for herself and she was better off here with Trudy and John. Her muscles relaxed. She wasn't doing anything wrong. Maybe Adam would get upset. But damnit, he wouldn't own her. She was quite capable of thinking for herself, and she had all the faith in the world that she could make good choices when it came to her own safety.

A calm resolve settled over her, and she drifted off to sleep.

It was still dark out when she woke up and realized she was alone in the bed. Voices drifted up the stairs from the living room, and she sat up, the covers nestled around her, listening.

John and Margo had company. She could smell the other werewolves. Her ears tickled while she strained to hear their words, something about a human meeting. The werewolves wanted John's permission to break it up.

"We need to take matters into our own hands," a woman said. She didn't recognize the voice but the female sounded determined. "We heard what they said. Those humans are bragging about capturing the werewolf leader."

"That means that Knight has failed us." A male werewolf said that, but Trudy had a hard time concentrating on the rest of the conversation.

"We don't have all of the facts." Margo sounded like she was trying to calm the werewolves down.

And this was true. She didn't have all of the facts. But Trudy had heard enough. If Adam had been captured then he needed help. She wouldn't lay around waiting for him to return if he was in trouble.

She found her clothes in the dark and dressed quickly. Thoughts of trying to sneak out of the house crossed her mind. But she wouldn't do that. More than likely John would try to stop her, but he wouldn't be able to. She was headed back to Adam's house. He could accompany her, find an escort, or let her go on her own. She didn't care. All Trudy knew was that she planned on heading out now. The sooner she could learn where Adam was, the sooner she could help him.

Chapter Twenty

"Absolutely not." John Campbell towered over her, his large stance making him more than menacing. His brow knit together while he stared at her as if she were out of her head. "I will not let you go back to Adam's house. It's not safe to run alone, and I have no one available to accompany you."

"I'm of no use to you here." Trudy would stay calm. Aggravation crept down her spine, its spiciness filling the air around her. "At least there I stand a chance of finding out where he went. Maybe I could contact his assistant."

That was the last thing she planned on doing.

"I've already spoken with Raven." John gave her a long, appraising look.

She didn't falter. And she wouldn't back down. What she said made sense. Whether she could get this alpha male to see that was another question. He turned to Margo, as if searching for help in reasoning with a female. Trudy rocked up on her toes.

"I take it she didn't give you any reassuring news." Trudy swallowed slowly when John returned his attention to her. She wouldn't let him intimidate her.

Margo almost looked like she would smile, but crossed her arms over her chest and managed to appear serious. Trudy had a feeling she was enjoying watching her mate be challenged.

And in all sincerity that wasn't what Trudy was trying to do. John was pack leader. She respected him. That was why she wasn't sneaking out when their backs were turned.

"Adam hasn't reported to her yet on his situation," he informed her. "And all that tells me is that the situation isn't resolved yet. I won't jump to conclusions over hearsay from humans."

"I don't accept that they are less intelligent simply because they are different from us." She'd had a lifetime of discrimination and she knew how it could fog someone's thinking.

John towered over her. His shirt stretched over broad shoulders while muscles rippled over his chest. His dark skin almost glowed while emotions surged through him. Long thick eyelashes hooded his dark stare. Her stomach flip-flopped. He was as good-looking as he was dangerous. A deadly combination.

But if he thought she would cower, he was mistaken. She straightened, meeting his stare, daring not to look away.

"No one is denying the intelligence of humans, my dear." His voice was so smooth it was almost hypnotic. "But I will acknowledge they are dangerous. They attack what they do not know, and what they fear."

"I know that," she hissed, worried if she didn't interrupt him she might fall into some trance staring into his handsome face.

Margo gave her a quick look, disapproving, a warning. She needed to remind herself that this was her new pack, Margo, her queen bitch. She lowered her head in respect.

"I need to know that he isn't hurt," she said quickly, keeping her eyes lowered. "If he needs help, I want to help him. I am fast, faster than your pack. I can escape any human who chases me."

"I know you want to help." John sounded calmer, less dangerous.

She dared to look up, glancing from him to Margo.

They were both so attractive, a damned sexy couple. She could seduce them, both of them. Their stares told her that they were interested in her, would fuck her if she let them. It wouldn't take much to lure them both into bed, distract them with lust, and get what she wanted. She ran her tongue over her upper lip, feeling her heart pound in her chest.

But she wouldn't do that. She didn't need to. "I need to help," she emphasized. "I can't sit around here watching television while your pack mates come over in anguish about these humans."

Margo moved closer to her mate, running her delicate fingers up the huge muscles in his arm. "None of us are going to go back to bed. It's almost light out anyway."

When John looked down at her she saw his expression relax. His gaze dropped to her arm, but then before she could react, he grabbed her hand, bringing it to his mouth. Trudy saw his teeth clamp down on one of Margo's fingers, not too hard, but she could swear she felt the slight pinch ride through her like a surge of electricity. Quick and sharp.

Margo sucked in her breath. Trudy caught herself doing the same thing.

"I can find tasks for her today," Margo offered.

John smiled. His look was dark and predatory though. It almost made Trudy shiver and she found she couldn't look away.

"Passion runs deep through you, my love." His voice was no more than a deep, gravelly whisper. "She will move you with her compassion and strong feelings for Adam. You will smell them on her and it will distract you."

"No." Margo shook her head. It looked like she watched her finger, which John still held against his lips.

"Yes." He squeezed her hand. Margo focused on his grip. "I will keep Trudy by my side today. She will work with me."

He let go of Margo's hand and she brought it to her chest, searching her mate's face. But she didn't argue with him, and she didn't look at Trudy. John turned and walked out of the room. A minute later, Trudy heard the shower water start in the bathroom.

If Margo had a problem with Trudy spending the day with her mate, she gave no indication of it. Things got busy pretty fast with the phone ringing, and pack members stopping by. Trudy managed a shower before John appeared at the door to his bedroom.

"Are you ready to go?" he asked.

She turned to question him, ask what it was that they would be doing, but he turned away, heading for the stairs. All she could do was hurry and grab her shoes and follow after him.

By the time she got downstairs, Margo stood at the front door, watching John head for his car.

"Don't worry." She smiled while Trudy struggled with her shoe. "He won't bite. Unless you want him too."

With her shoes finally tied, Trudy followed John out the front door, making a face at Margo, but otherwise not commenting. She wasn't sure what to say. Margo gave her rear end a friendly slap, making her jump. Margo giggled.

"Seems to me his mate has a bigger bite than he does," she said over her shoulder.

Margo gave her a broad grin and Trudy couldn't help but smile back. "Don't you worry. I'll keep him out of trouble."

"Good luck." Margo waved then shut the door.

By the end of the morning, she had a good idea of what it was like to be a newspaper reporter. No one in his hectic office, a large room with rows of desks and humans moving around constantly, seemed to care that she was with him. In fact, no one paid any attention to her at all.

She sat opposite him, facing his desk, while he went over email and voice mail, and sorted through his inbox.

"I'd forgotten you were a reporter," she murmured, although it didn't matter how quietly she spoke. There was enough noise going on around them that it would have been difficult for the humans to narrow in on their conversation.

"Being pack leader doesn't pay the mortgage." He winked at her.

She began analyzing John Campbell while she sat there, watching him interact with humans, manage to calm and cheer all those around him. A true alpha male, in control, assertive, and a leader. It startled her that he led the humans, instead of sticking to himself, but he did. More than one of them approached him throughout the morning with questions, comments, seeking out his advice, or his approval.

"Are you in charge here?" she asked, after the third human had sought him out for his opinion.

He seemed surprised. "We all have the same rank." He shrugged. "We're reporters."

"They look up to you." She glanced around, not seeing anyone else who seemed to rank among the lot.

"I'm good." He had a winning smile, his eyes charming and friendly when he wanted them to be.

She found herself relaxing, leaning back in the chair, even handing him items on the desk while he spoke on the phone, or implied he needed something.

Once, his cell phone rang while he was on the phone. He nodded for her to answer, leaning back and scratching his goatee while he discussed a local issue going on in the town.

"Hello." She listened to the excited voice on the other end. "Slow down. I need to write this down."

Grabbing one of the many legal pads scattered over his desk, Trudy reached for a pen, and began taking notes. John's call ended before hers and he leaned forward, reading upside down while she wrote.

"Tell him we're on our way."

"We're on our way," she told the werewolf, after noting the address of a house that had caught fire earlier that morning. Several werewolves were now displaced, and although the pack had jumped in and no one was hurt, foul play was suspected.

John's phone rang before they were out of the building. "Hello," he said, his voice deep and more dangerous sounding than when he spoke to humans.

Trudy glanced up at him.

"Is anyone home out there?" He scowled, reaching over her head when they reached the exit, and holding the door open for her.

She squinted against the midday sun.

"What's wrong?" she asked once in his car.

"Two house fires this morning. The second one is still burning." John merged into traffic, immediately hurrying around slower cars. "We're headed out there now."

When his phone rang again, the tone was different. "Hi babe," he answered, his face still showing his frustration, but his tone softer.

Trudy guessed the call was Margo. The excited voice coming through on the other end tickled her ear. Frustration filled the inside of the small car.

"I know of two houses." He paused. "Calm down. So there are four?"

Again Margo's excited tones crept through although Trudy couldn't hear what she said.

"I agree. It doesn't look good." After a minute he added. "Okay. Have the pack check in. I'll contact Werewolf Affairs."

He hung up the phone, dropping it between them, and slammed his fist against the steering wheel. Trudy jumped, watching him while emotions raced across his face. His handsome features were chiseled in stone, other than a nerve that twitched along his jawbone. The spicy smell of anger, mixed with frustration, almost made her sneeze.

Her heart throbbed painfully while her stomach tied in knots.

"What is Werewolf Affairs?" She knew this had something to do with Adam, and had to know what was going on.

John glanced over at her, his look intimidating. Heat rushed over her but she held her ground. His watching her unnerved her. Margo said he wouldn't bite, but he sure could if he wanted to. But if she could stand up to Adam, then she could stand up to this werewolf. He wouldn't keep secrets from her, not if it involved Adam. She had to know.

He seemed to sense that. "It's a branch of the FBI. I'm sure you know already that Adam works for them."

She nodded, staring forward. Something was terribly wrong and the instinct to run raced through her. So much more could be accomplished in her fur, instead of moving slowly in her human form.

"Why are you going to contact them?" The painful lump in her chest made it hard to breathe.

"Because it appears the humans are burning us out." His answer scared her, cold sweat breaking out under her clothes. He paused for a moment before adding, "and it appears that Adam hasn't succeeded in killing their leader."

She looked over at him, understanding his anger. The situation frustrated him, but not knowing what was going on with Adam bothered him more. The werewolves were friends, obviously good friends if John had shared his mate with him. She guessed John wished he could go find Adam, help him if needed. But his hands were tied. He was pack leader, and his duties were here.

"Let me go find him," she whispered.

John turned a corner, and it took her a minute to realize they had gone to his house. He pulled into the drive, hopping out as the front door opened. Margo looked as upset as he did.

"Okay." John turned to her once they were inside. "You may go."

Trudy thought her heart would explode. "I won't let you down," she promised, and meant it. She wouldn't stop until she was with Adam.

"We know you won't." Margo reached for her, her touch warm. Her soft brown eyes filled with worry and Trudy squeezed her hand, a silent reassurance.

"There are stipulations." John's baritone caught her attention.

"What?" She didn't let go of Margo but focused on the pack leader. He seemed to have grown since they arrived at his house.

"You drive to his house. I want you to stay in your skin."

Immediately she wanted to protest. She was stronger, faster in her fur.

He raised his hand. With his fingers spread it was almost the size of her face.

"When you get there, you call me," he continued, his dark eyes watching her, noting her reaction to his words, sensing her emotions.

She had no doubt he knew her thoughts without her voicing them. John Campbell would not be a good werewolf to have as an enemy. She relaxed, nodding.

"And once you are there, I want you to search his place and see if you can find out where he went."

His last words startled her. Margo gave him a quick look as well. He turned on them though, leaving the room. Margo took a step to follow him but he returned in the next minute.

"Once you have the information, use this phone to call me." He gave her a cellular phone. "My number is programmed in it."

Trudy wanted to know what would happen once she called him with the information. But she didn't want to hear him forbid her to go after him. Margo's curiosity wasn't as easily appeased.

"We're going to go find him. Right?" Her expression glowed. She was up for the adventure just like Trudy was.

"Pack leaders do not interfere with Werewolf Affairs." His tone was stern, his expression revealing nothing.

But she wasn't pack leader, nor was she queen bitch. She fought a grin, eager to get on the road.

"I'll call you as soon as I get there." She glanced from one of them to the other, not even daring to think what she would do after she learned where he was.

Hugging both of them, she turned and headed for her car.

Chapter Twenty-One

Adam studied the door to his prison, the soft dirt underneath him cold and damp. He'd pissed Christopher Hordan off earlier. Whatever his reasons, the human despised werewolves. But what really puzzled Adam was that it appeared the human had werewolf blood in him.

Searching his memory, recalling the childhood tales, he wondered at the truth in them. In all of his years with the Bureau, he'd never heard of the two species reproducing together. Obviously humans and werewolves could have sex. In his human form he could fuck a human as easily as he could fuck a werewolf. The idea had never crossed his mind though. Humans didn't appeal to him.

But there were werewolves who sought out humans. It would be risky. He would think the distraction of keeping emotions at bay so the beast didn't surface would be too distracting to enjoy the sex. Not his idea of a good time.

But the chances of a werewolf and human conceiving together had to be slim if not close to impossible. Yet he'd seen two humans inside that house who obviously had werewolf blood in them.

He needed answers. Sitting here was getting him nowhere. His cell was almost airtight, but what smells lingered through the closed door told him it was night. Closing his eyes, he concentrated on his breathing. It wouldn't do him any good at the moment to change completely, but he was tired of his handcuffs.

His heartbeat accelerated, blood rushing through his veins, the muscles around his bones contorting, strengthening. He bit his lip, his teeth slightly longer and more pointed than a second ago. Focusing on the slight pain, running his tongue over the bitter taste of blood, he fought to keep his senses about him, prevent the change from rippling through him completely.

His muscles strained around the handcuffs, pain rippling through him as his wrists thickened, pressed against the muscles. In the next minute the metal popped, torn apart while his body continued to grow.

Humans were talking in the yard outside. His heightened senses picked up on their words, his ears itching, twitching to catch what was said.

"None of that matters now." Hordan's voice sounded angry, the walls of his cell too thick for him to smell emotions. "Everything is going as planned. More than likely they will start a mass exodus and then we can catch them on the run."

"Best to get them out of the towns," a male human added.

What didn't matter now? And why did Hordan think the werewolves would start a mass exodus? Adam brought his wrists together, his heartbeat pulsating where the metal had cut his skin. The thickness of his body made it harder to move like a human. But he wanted to hear what they said. Half-changed, he could take advantage of better sight and vision. Changing all the way right now wouldn't work. He needed to stay here as long as possible to learn as much as he could. If he changed, they would assume he meant to escape, and he wasn't ready to leave yet.

"Father!" The female's voice perked his ears up. "We've found Knight's house."

Adam felt a steel sword stab straight through his heart. He held his breath until it hurt, needing to hear what was said next. They couldn't get to Trudy, unless she disarmed the security system.

"Do you think he can't hear you?" Christopher hissed. "That brick cage doesn't confine his senses. And it won't confine him either if he hears something that forces him to change."

Adam edged across the dirt floor, pressing his ear to the door. Blood surged through him, creating a ringing in his head. Everything that he was ached to change and lunge through the door, protect what was his. The instinct rushed through him like hot lava, burning and powerful.

"Well, then put him in a stronger cage." Silence followed her defiant tone.

Adam could only imagine what actions might be taking place on the other side of his brick and mortar cell.

"Where is his house?" Christopher spoke much quieter, forcing Adam to strain to hear.

"Not far from here. But it gets better, Father. There is a woman there."

Adam swore he could smell her sick pleasure over her finding. His stomach turned. If any of them lay a hand on Trudy, they would die. He couldn't stay here any longer. The Bureau wanted more information on Hordan, a history, a motive, a list of all involved. But his instincts wouldn't stay at bay, not if Trudy was in danger.

Adam heard footsteps. They faded quickly. More than likely Christopher guided his daughter out of the yard to discuss his plans. The human knew quite a bit about the abilities of werewolves, and Adam's guess was because he was part werewolf himself.

He circled twice in his small confinement before realizing his animal needs were consuming his human rationale.

Protect Trudy. Keep the humans away from her.

The Bureau had sent him out here to find the werewolf killer, learn what he could about him, and bring him down. He'd come this far. Now somehow he needed to buy time and finish his assignment. But he also needed to know that Trudy was safe.

No other humans came out into the backyard. He'd been left alone. An hour passed. Maybe more. He only knew that darkness surrounded him. The smells of night seeped through the walls of his prison. Humans weren't nocturnal and he would use that to his advantage.

He slipped out of the pants Mary had given him and let the change consume him. It felt so good. After restraining all this time, holding in his carnal instincts, keeping his raw emotions at bay, to allow them all to release was a pure soul cleansing.

The door to his prison fell to the ground, cold night air rushing around him, the sweet smell of the trees cleansing his senses. He stepped out of the small brick dwelling, nothing more than a huge box, more than likely built just to hold werewolves.

Better build a stronger cage.

Taking a minute to look around him, get his bearings, he determined there were no humans around. He found that strange. Someone so intent on killing off an entire race of beings would surely have security around his home.

All he could do was store the information. Right now, he had a mission to finish, and his woman to protect. He would not allow Trudy to be hurt.

One thing bothered him. At least two of the humans here had werewolf blood in them. He would learn the details around that knowledge. But if these humans weren't opposed to mating with werewolves, how would they treat Trudy?

Fire burned through him with such intensity he couldn't return to his human form. Primitive emotions too raw for any human to handle consumed him with a fever he couldn't appease. Just the thought that one of them might touch her, try to seduce her, or in any way make sexual advances toward her sent a feeling of outrage through him that he'd never experienced before.

For right now though, he needed to secure the house, find out who was here and who wasn't, learn their plans. That could only be done in his skin. Pain ripped through him this time while he returned to his human form, forcing the emotions that struggled inside him to ebb, at least for now.

Grabbing his pants, he struggled into them while making his way across the yard. Damp grass soaked his feet, the dew hanging heavy in the air. His predator's instincts held strong within him, every dark shadow grabbing his attention, the shift of the breeze keeping him alert.

A beeping sounded when he opened the back door. An alarm had been triggered. Keeping his breathing slow, focusing the best he could with his human eyes in the darkness, he smelled the air. There were humans here. Or at least their smell was strong enough that they'd been here recently. He wasn't sure.

Footsteps sounded upstairs. At the same time someone stirred in the living area. The alarm must have woken them.

It appeared he would be securing the area first and gathering information later. Adam moved into the shadows, waiting to see which human would approach him first. Slipping into the living room, he spotted the human male with beady eyes who had helped escort him to Hordan earlier.

"Werewolf, is that you?" He had a guttural tone, deep and raspy. "Get tired of your cramped quarters?"

Adam heard a gun cock. Shifting his attention to the stairs, he saw the younger guard approach, the one with the lingering scent of werewolf about him.

"Porter, are you okay?" The human werewolf reached the bottom of the stairs.

"He's here in the living room." Porter still sounded raspy, maybe a cold. He didn't smell of cigarettes. "We've got him trapped though."

"Don't get cocky," the human snapped. "Don't ever assume you've got the upper hand when it comes to a werewolf."

He moved into view, a large rifle poised right at Adam. The distinct werewolf scent was strong surrounding the man. Adam studied him, noticing the dilated pupils and thick jaw. The young human had changed partially to accommodate the darkness. His senses were heightened. Adam wondered if he had enough control over himself that he allowed the partial change, or if his emotions just ran too strong for his human form.

"And how is it that you are the werewolf expert?" Adam asked him, watching the human adjust his grip on his rifle. He raised it so Adam stared down the length of it.

"That is none of your fucking business." Anger wrapped around the man, his fingers gripping the trigger.

He would shoot. Whatever his motives to destroy the bloodline he partially came from, he would shoot. Adam knew the look of a man intent on killing. And this young man didn't look like he would hesitate.

Adam didn't take his gaze off the young man with his rifle pointed steady at his face. He didn't blink, and gave no indication of his next move. Quicker than either human could react, he dropped to his knees, grabbing the underside of the dining room table, and lifting it sideways.

Chairs toppled over. The sudden noise startled both men. In that split second it took them to react to his sudden movement, he flipped the table, throwing it toward the older human.

Shots fired in the air. Plaster showered down on them. One of them had fired at the ceiling. Upstairs, a woman began screaming. A bloodcurdling sound that rang through Adam's ears.

"If you've hurt her," the young human screamed. "I'll kill you, if you've hurt her."

The female upstairs didn't stop her commotion. The noise obviously affected both men. Adam jumped over the sideways table, grabbing one of the chairs and flinging it at the younger human, while he lunged at the older one. A fist to the side of the head, and the older human with the gravelly voice collapsed to the ground. Adam grabbed his gun, and turned on the younger man who had half-changed into a werewolf.

Standing like a human, but with legs now incapable of being straight, he hunched over, his spine twisted in its half-werewolf, half-human shape.

"I'm going to enjoy killing you." His voice was barely audible, dagger-like teeth pressing hard against his still human lips.

Realizing his hands could barely hold the rifle, the human werewolf threw the gun, screaming in a rage. Adam took advantage of his fit and lunged at him, throwing all of his strength into his attack.

"Why would you want to kill your own kind?" he hissed, falling forward on top of the younger man.

He tossed the rifle he had in his hand and grabbed the thickened neck of his opponent.

"You are not one of my kind." The growled words curdled in the man's throat, constricted from Adam's grip.

Surprise seemed to overcome the warped features on the man's face when he couldn't overcome Adam.

Adam hit him hard, a blow to the temple, and the human relaxed underneath him, his human features taking over. Within a minute, no sign of the werewolf existed.

Adam stood, listening. The female upstairs whimpered, but otherwise the house grew deathly quiet. If anyone else was here, they were waiting to attack or too scared to come out.

Chapter Twenty-Two

Adam stepped over the unconscious human and headed toward the stairs. Once he had the house secure, he needed to contact Werewolf Affairs before they sent out the cavalry. The boss didn't like to be left in the dark. Adam had pushed his time frame to the limit; he needed to check in.

At the top of the stairs, he looked down an open hallway, several closed doors on either side except for one room. Its door was opened and the whimpering female sounded like she came from in there.

Not much surprised Adam. He'd seen things that would turn the strongest werewolf's stomach. But it took a minute for him to quit staring when he paused in the open doorway.

"Are you okay?" he asked the young woman who knelt on all fours, chained to the wall.

She was beautiful. More than beautiful, she was stunning, breathtaking. Long black hair floated over her naked body, barely covering large firm breasts. Each nipple was pierced, silver loops embedded with jewels adorning the dark brown areolas. Tattoos covered her body, a bright red detailed rose pattern covering her hip and traipsing over her exposed ass.

She watched him with oversized black eyes, thick lashes fluttering, blinking quickly showing her nervousness. Her full lips, more red than they should be, didn't stretch over her extended jowl. Her sharpened teeth were barely covered by her sensuous full lips. A long dark tail flitted between her legs, dusting the floor with its worried twitch.

Any man would be captivated by the submissive image before him. On all fours, staring up at him, with a studded collar around her neck, a thin chain attached to a large metal loop on the wall. Her sexuality saturated the room, a rich full smell, branded into the walls as if this had been her home for many years.

"I'm not going to hurt you." He felt like a father approaching a terrified child.

And in all essence he guessed that was what he was doing. Even though this woman was no child, her body displayed before him like a seasoned whore, she looked up at him with the fearful gaze of an innocent.

Whimpering, she backed up onto a large feather-stuffed pillow. The chain around her neck allowed the movement, and her graceful actions showed she was very accustomed to her confinement.

"What's your name, Miss?" He moved closer, scanning her body with his eyes, seeing no blood, smelling no pain. She was simply scared. The noises downstairs obviously had terrified her.

"Darla can't talk." Christopher Hordan leaned in the doorway behind him.

Adam turned quickly, chastising himself for having been so distracted he'd allowed his senses to lower.

"She's a damned good fuck though." Christopher smiled; he nudged his glasses up his nose with his finger. In his other hand, he held a small pistol with a silencer attached. "She can suck some damned good cock, too."

He chuckled, the sound almost sinister.

"And like the rest of you, she is half-werewolf." Adam watched closely for Christopher's reaction.

The man ignored the comment.

"We tried to educate her when she was a child, but all she learned to do well was spread her legs. She likes it, so we indulge her." His grin turned sinister. "She will do anything you want her to do. Care to give her a try?"

Adam saw no reason to acknowledge the insulting comment.

Christopher snorted. "I didn't think so. You would probably upset your mate, who I'm sure is dying to know when you will return to her."

Adam didn't like the way Christopher mentioned Trudy. Knowledge gleamed in the man's green eyes.

A phone rang in the other room and Christopher gestured with his gun. "This way, werewolf. I'm sure this is the call I've been waiting for."

Adam moved toward the doorway. Darla whimpered behind him and he turned to look at her.

Christopher stamped his foot on the ground. "Silence, Darla," he ordered.

She went mute, curling her body like a dog would on to her pillow, her cheek resting on her hands. It was amazing how innocent those oversized dark eyes were that stared at him. Her luscious body betrayed that innocence, making her a contradiction he couldn't grasp.

"If you give me the information I want, maybe I'll let her suck your dick later." Christopher laughed, grabbing Adam's arm and pushing him toward the ringing phone.

It crossed his mind to attack, to knock the pompous look right off of this crazed man's face. But he was curious about the phone call, and also wondered what information the human wanted from him. The more he could tell the Bureau when he checked in, the less chance he would have of getting a reprimand for not contacting them sooner.

Dark shadows fell across the large master room that Christopher Hordan shoved Adam into. He took a quick minute to look around, taking in the elaborate furniture, the thick carpet under his feet, and the dark sinister oil paintings hanging on the walls.

Images of witch hangings from the Salem trials, graphic scenes of slaughtered villagers from a time gone by, razzings of blacks in the deep South, covered Christopher Hordan's walls. The paintings were large, framed in heavy gold frames, the thick layers of bright oils on canvas adding to the gross intensity of each scene. Adam glanced from one to the other, realizing each picture displayed a scene where the masses were attempting to wipe out a fear they didn't understand.

But in each case, history had proven that it had been wrong to kill these people. What kind of madness weaved through Hordan's mind that he didn't see that?

"What?" Hordan grabbed the cordless phone, which rested on the nightstand next to his bed. He lowered his gun, apparently confident that Adam wouldn't try anything, although his gaze never left him.

The excited female voice on the other end of the line tickled Adam's ears. He focused, trying to hear what she said, although her words were muffled.

"What?" Christopher almost shouted. "You allowed her to escape?"

Silence hung heavy in the room. Adam struggled to hear what was being said but Christopher held the phone too close to his head.

The crazed look didn't fade from his gaze when he narrowed it on Adam. He raised his gun toward him.

"Let her come. Head back this way. She will play right into my plan." He actually chuckled when he hung up the phone, then without blinking an eye, he shot Adam.

Adam cursed himself for relaxing in the presence of a madman. Curiosity had gotten the best of him, and it had gotten him shot. His tongue seemed stuck to his mouth while he blinked several times, struggling to focus. Whatever Hordan had shot him with, it hadn't been designed to knock him out for very long. His thoughts were in a cloud, but with some effort, he was able to clear them.

It did take him a moment to realize his positioning. He was standing against the wall, his arms manacled in heavy iron shackles, the kind found in museums used in another time. They were heavy, strong, and he couldn't move his wrists. Quite possibly he could hurt himself if he changed under such severe confinement.

Glancing down, he realized his ankles were shackled together too. But that wasn't what grabbed his attention. Darla kneeled in front of him, her dark eyes looking up at him with pure fascination.

"She's never done a purebred werewolf before." Christopher sounded amused. "I think she is rather excited."

Adam stared over at the insane human who reclined in an overstuffed chair, a drink in his hand. He sipped the golden liquid, whiskey Adam guessed by the smell. To the side of the room, the two guards lay crumpled on the floor. Christopher showed no signs of caring that they lay there, unconscious.

"Darla." Christopher snapped his fingers and the female stood, turning to him. "Give him something to drink."

He picked up another glass that sat on the coffee table in front of him. Early morning shadows crept across the room, which otherwise wasn't lit. Darla moved to take the glass, her long thick tail swaying behind her, almost touching the ground when she walked. He noticed her toes curled, unlike a human's, but otherwise she held all the grace and exotic behavior of a skilled courtesan.

She turned, glass in hand, and smiled at him. Her incisors extended to her lower lip but appeared to have been filed. He could guess the reason why. Those full luscious lips would beckon most men, but dagger-like teeth would hinder her abilities to please. She ran her tongue over her upper lip, seemingly aware that her captive audience had eyes only for her.

Adam flexed his wrists against the steel wristbands holding him to the wall. Blood rushed through him, the urgency to break free and end this charade overwhelming him. He'd heard what Christopher said on the phone. Trudy had escaped. The only way they would be able to catch her would be to shoot her. The need to protect surged through him, forcing his muscles to grow and press painfully against his shackles.

Darla made a gurgling sound in her throat while she raked a fingernail over the front of his thigh. She didn't break skin but pressed hard enough to make him flinch, the action dangerously close to his cock.

"She doesn't like to be ignored when she is with a man." Christopher sounded amused.

Adam realized he'd had his eyes closed, concentrating so intently on his next move that he'd managed to block her out.

"I'm sure she doesn't," he mumbled, glancing down at her.

Her studded piercings covered the roundness of her nipples, keeping them hard, puckered, eager to be played with. The fullness of her breasts complimented the jewelry, while her narrow waist and flat tummy implied her fragility. Completely shaved, her pussy graced a tattoo, a vine pattern covered with small roses that disappeared around her hips. He already knew the tattoo spread over part of her ass.

"But tell me." He dared to glance away from the mutant seductress. "Why did you change your mind?"

Christopher raised an eyebrow. "I don't believe I've changed my mind about anything."

Adam looked down at the woman who stood before him. Darla pressed up against him, no fear in those dark eyes. Her smile was warm, content. In her simpleness, she assumed he wanted her. Her fingernails grazed over his skin while her small hand stroked his chest. She leaned into him, pressing her large breasts against his skin until he could feel her tiny heart pitter-pattering against his flesh. It beat too fast for a human.

She grunted, her lips parting, while she held the glass to his lips. He kept his gaze on her while he sipped, the whiskey burning all the way down. The hardness of the glass clinked against his teeth before she pulled it away. Her lips formed a small circle, fascination in her expression. Her emotions were so pure, so open, every reaction she had to him was like an infant discovering something for the first time. In all her beauty, all her adorned nakedness, he wasn't attracted to her. She needed to be rescued and taken care of, not fucked.

Adam looked over her head, grateful that his mouth no longer felt like sandpaper. The headiness of the alcohol actually helped clear his head, and he wondered if Christopher had actually offered the whiskey with that intent, wanting him clearheaded while he endured the twisted torture awaiting him.

"You told me if I gave you the information that you wanted, you would allow this beautiful creature to suck my cock." He hoped he sounded interested, that the thought of this house whore offering such a treat had him willing to do anything.

The human werewolf had a serious expression on his face, appearing to stare at Darla's ass but not seeing it. It was as if his thoughts distracted him.

"You are going to tell me what I want to know, trust me."

He wouldn't trust this man as far as he could throw him. And at the moment, hurling him against the wall had its appeal.

"What is it that you want to know?" If he kept the conversation on business, he stood a better chance of enduring Darla.

"Everything that you know," Christopher answered, leaning forward. "Darla. Suck his cock."

Darla once again knelt in front of him, placing the glass on the floor by her side. Her fingers brushed over his stomach, her touch gentle while her nails grazed his skin, giving him chills. She rested her hand on the elastic of his pants, looking up at him, searching his expression with those large dark eyes.

"You don't have to do this," he told her gently, wondering how much she understood.

"She wants to do it." Christopher answered for her and Adam thought he saw her cower just a bit, her attention gone from his face and intent on her actions.

"Why is she like this?" Adam was all too aware of her lowering his pants, revealing his cock, her fingers all over it instantly. He hated that he would have to disappoint her and not get hard.

"Like what?" Christopher sipped at his drink. "A slut? Do you think she could get a job as a secretary?" His words were hard, cold bitterness filling the air while he revealed his inept bitterness that she was the way she was.

Adam glanced down when she put her full lips over his cockhead. Her tongue darted around him, tasting him. Those extended teeth, dulled from a file, pressed against his sensitive flesh, demanding his attention momentarily. He fought not to suck in a breath. The gentle roughness of her teeth, with the moist softness of those full lips, was a combination made to drive a man wild. Darla was very good at what she was doing.

He raised his head, needing a distraction. Blood pumped hard through his body while he exerted every bit of his energy to stay focused and not allow her very personal torture session to affect him.

Glancing across the room at the two human guards, still crumpled on the floor, and then back at Hordan, who sat with a sneer on his face, he wondered when Trudy would show up.

"When Darla first sucked cock, she did a very bad thing." His voice seemed to drift through the air. "Accidentally, she bit off the man's cock."

Adam's heart quit pumping. For a moment he couldn't breathe. The restraints around his wrists and ankles seemed to tighten. Darla's gentle caresses suddenly made him feel numb.

"Well, it proved a wonderful discovery," Hordan continued. "And since I hate to administer pain, I will simply sit here, enjoying this good whiskey, while you tell me everything that you know. And you get the pleasure of a blow job out of the deal."

Christopher Hordan began laughing. His sick sense of humor clogged the air with a putrid smell, leaving a foul taste in Adam's mouth. Twisting his wrists against the metal, he stared down at Darla. She looked up at him, those oversized dark eyes wide and unblinking while she sucked him into her mouth. Hot moist lips, then dull teeth, taking him in, his shaft disappearing as she consumed him.

"Tell me the names of pack leaders." Hordan's voice turned cold, steely, his animosity chilling the air. "I want names and the city they are located in."

"Fuck you." Adam's words garbled, the change seeping through him. He couldn't wait to get his hands around this sick human's throat.

Darla ran her fingers up his chest, her thick black hair tickling his groin while she stroked his cock with her mouth. Fire burned through him, her actions having an impact on him while his outrage encouraged the change.

"You would be surprised how loyal my dear Darla is to me." Hordan had lowered his voice to a mere whisper, an evil, loathing whisper. "One word from me and she will bite your cock off without giving it a thought."

Adam wasn't sure who screamed first when a sudden explosion filled the air, its crashing sound riveting through him.

Chapter Twenty-Three

For a second, Adam thought Darla had bitten his cock clear through. Pain riveted through him so quickly it took a moment to realize he was falling. Muscles expanded so quickly through him he barely felt the pain as he ripped through his shackles. Landing on all fours, he lunged at the white ball of fur that attacked Christopher Hordan.

No! Don't kill him! He snarled at Trudy, doing his best to try and calm his savage little bitch.

Much to his surprise, she turned on him, baring her teeth, her long white fangs ready to do deadly damage. Furious or not, Trudy was alive and obviously not injured, which was a damn good thing considering she had just plunged through the living room window sending shattered glass everywhere.

He wanted to press against her, relish in the feel of her silky coat, assure her that everything was okay. Her rich scent surrounded her, soothing his outrage. She calmed his nerves just knowing she was alive and not captured.

Still snarling, she circled him, almost as if she needed reassurance that he was okay. He turned, not willing to let her out of his view. Her slender body, the sleekness of her coat when she moved, her intense silver eyes, every bit of her was a sight for sore eyes. She sniffed at his cock, her moist nose rushing life through him faster than he anticipated.

But then she turned her attention on Darla. The human werewolf had jumped to the side of the room, on her haunches next to one of the unconscious guards. Her long black tail curled up between her legs, covering her shaved pussy, fluttering nervously over her flat tummy. Her long black hair covered most of her nudity, but she had brushed it back from her face, those oversized eyes staring at the two of them with fear and wonder.

Trudy's tail swished, darting angrily from one side of her to the other. She approached Darla, her head lowered, her hackles rising over her shoulder blades. Adam saw quickly if he didn't take charge of the situation, he would have an even bigger mess on his hands.

The change didn't come easily to him. Strong emotions made returning to his skin a challenge. Anger, frustration, desire all tore through him with the intensity of a winter's wind. This mission needed to be tied together, answers given to the Bureau and matters put to rest. But with Trudy here, his protector's instincts fought to take over.

"Trudy. No." He spoke as soon as his mouth could form words.

She turned on him, looking up with her teeth bared. Straightening, her face transforming while fur receded into her flesh, and her almond-shaped silver eyes growing rounder and a pale blue, she glared at him, her mouth moving before she could speak.

"I saw through the window," she managed to growl, her words hindered by fangs that continued to shorten while she spoke.

There would be questions, many questions, but now wasn't the time to answer them. He turned to Hordan, checking for a pulse. It was weak, but the human was alive. Stepping gingerly in his bare feet, working to avoid shattered glass, he checked the two guards, grateful to see both of them were alive also.

Darla darted around him, trying to touch him.

"Hands off," Trudy snarled, glaring at the crouched woman. "Touch him and you'll regret it."

Darla cowered, babbling something in a whimpering tone.

"Why doesn't she pick a form?" Trudy studied her, her breasts heaving while she continued to breathe heavily.

He could only imagine how fast she ran to get here, and the amount of adrenaline she exerted to break through that window. Her blonde hair clung to her, moist from sweat. She looked so damned sexy that for a moment all he could do was stare, willing her nipples to pucker while he watched.

"I'm not sure that she can," he told her, reaching for her, taking her small hand in his. "Come on. I doubt we have much time."

Her touch spawned desire in him stronger than he anticipated. She'd mastered a daring feat to rescue him, and she'd done a damned good job. The heat from her palm sizzled through him, his groin tightening, walking becoming a challenge.

Trudy pushed against him, clinging to his hand when they reached the top of the stairs. He led her to Christopher Hordan's room and headed for the phone.

To say Werewolf Affairs was happy to hear from him was an understatement. Trudy watched him wide-eyed while he relayed the events to his superior that had happened since he'd been captured.

"The place is secure for the moment," he reported. "But I anticipate Hordan's followers showing up at any minute."

"That was the werewolf killer downstairs?" Trudy's pallor went ashy white.

Adam couldn't help but pull her into his arms, feel her flesh against his. He stroked her back, wanting to feel all of her at once, aching to bury himself deep inside her.

"And I will have to report that you are the one who took him down," he whispered into her hair. "That might make you a hero among the packs."

She looked up at him, amusement making her cheeks flush a luscious pink. "It seems pretty clear to me that you did most of the work."

He held her close, her heartbeat pulsating through him, her breath hot against his flesh, her scent swimming through his senses soothing him and driving him mad all at once.

Glancing over her head, he noticed Darla, hovering in the doorway, looking very much like a lost child.

"Go to your room, Darla," he told the woman.

Apparently she understood because she turned, her gaze lingering over both of them before she disappeared.

There were questions in Trudy's eyes when she looked up at him. "It's like she is stuck in a half-changed state," she muttered, "a child in a woman's body."

He thought of Hordan's threat to have Darla bite his cock off if he didn't offer information, and had a hard time seeing Darla as a child—more like a deadly weapon.

"You showed up in the nick of time." He stroked her cheek, brushing his lips over her forehead, tasting her, craving more of her instantly.

"Seems to me I could have shown up a bit sooner." Her lips puckered, her expression scolding.

He smiled. "If you'd shown up a few minutes later that little temptress might have bitten off my cock."

Trudy made a choking sound, her hand instantly moving to his hard cock pressed between them. She almost strangled all will power out of him when she delicately wrapped her fingers around him, stroking, pulling him closer to her.

"We don't have much time," he growled, telling himself that more than her.

But he had to have a bit of her, claim her all over again, if only for just a minute.

"I know you told me to stay at your house," she began, but explanations could be saved for later.

He nibbled on her lower lip, the moan that escaped her breathed fire through his tormented system. Maybe he was a bit too rough. Fire burned through him making it hard to think. Her flesh was so soft. He ran his hands down her back, over her ass, up her sides under her arms. Everywhere. He had to touch her everywhere.

Trudy leaned into him, pulling on his cock. He gripped her hair with one hand. Even damp it was so silky, he could imagine it brushing over him, stroking his body with its smooth touch. She opened her mouth to him and he dove into her. Rough. He didn't care anymore. The taste of her was so sweet, like nectar. Her moans vibrated through him, about sending him over the edge.

Maybe it was because his senses were overexcited. But a click downstairs hit him as loud as a gunshot. He raised his head, listening. The sound of Trudy struggling to catch her breath, while her heart pounded against his chest, almost drowned out what he wanted to hear.

"We have company," he whispered.

Trudy's body went stiff.

In the other room, Darla began howling, possibly warning whoever was here of their presence. The strong smell of humans drifted through the house. Adam pressed Trudy behind him, willing her to stay quiet with a look, and headed toward the bedroom door.

They could hear voices, concerned and scared. The human female, Mary, had picked up a phone downstairs, and Adam glanced at the phone alongside Christopher Hordan's bed. He would love to know who Hordan's daughter turned to in a time of crisis.

"They have guns," Trudy whispered, overhearing some of the conversation downstairs. "We need to change to protect ourselves."

Adam moved over to the bed, reaching for the phone. He gripped Trudy's wrist, feeling her heart pound through the slender bones in her arm. "I'll protect you," he snarled, but relaxed his grip when he saw the worry on her face. Her warm sweet aroma mixed with panic. "It's okay. There are werewolves on their way, and only a few of them downstairs."

He put his fingers to his lips, gesturing for her to stay quiet, and lifted the receiver. Someone started climbing the stairs though, causing him to curse silently. Placing the receiver back down as quietly as he had lifted it, he pulled

Trudy's warm body to his, her puckered nipples pressing against his skin.

"Shut up, Darla." Mary sounded aggravated. "Werewolf? Are you up here?"

Apparently her phone call hadn't taken that long. And she didn't seem too concerned with being quiet, her boots making a dull thud with each step over the carpet.

The sound of a helicopter approaching outside grabbed Adam's attention. He looked down at Trudy and smiled. "Werewolf Affairs has sent backup."

She looked confused for only a moment before glancing toward the window, the whirly sound growing louder. Within a few seconds it sounded like the thing would land on the roof.

"What the hell?" Mary cursed. "Werewolf? Where are you? Look. I won't hurt you. Come out and talk to me."

He moved toward the door, keeping Trudy behind him, which proved a small effort suddenly. She pushed against him, either instinct telling her to go after this female, or curiosity making her want to see over his shoulder.

"You took down three armed men downstairs," Mary continued, a slight panicked edge sounding in her voice. "I know I'm no match for you."

The sound of movement outside told him several werewolves had been let down out of the helicopter. They were securing the area.

"Come out. Look." Mary spoke faster, probably suspecting that her home was about to be invaded. He heard a thud in the hallway. "See? I've put down my gun. Talk to me, werewolf."

Why she was so desperate to talk to him, he had no clue. He moved into the doorway, seeing her a second before she turned and met his gaze. In a flash, she reached to scoop up her gun, fury burning in her bloodshot eyes. Her expression was contorted with raw anger.

Letting go of Trudy, he lunged at Mary, pouncing on her before she could get to her gun.

"No!" she screamed.

He straddled her, pressing her face into the carpet while he pinned her hands behind her back. Then he lifted her, not too nicely, her feet almost leaving the ground.

"I hate you! All of you!" She turned and spit at Trudy, her gaze traveling down Trudy's nude body in disgust. "Everything is your fault."

Adam had no idea what she was talking about, but he planned on finding out real soon.

Chapter Twenty-Four

It seemed she couldn't keep her hands off of him. Trudy returned to the couch, her full glass of wine in one hand, and sat on the arm, immediately running her fingers along Adam's shoulder.

Powerful taut muscles moved against her touch, his body warm through the soft material of his shirt. Even relaxed and reclined on the couch, his long legs spread out comfortably in front of him, he seemed alert, ready to jump into action on a moment's notice. Maybe he would always be that way.

"And every time these humans bred, werewolf characteristics came out in their young?" John Campbell sat across from them in Adam's living room, leaning forward, fascination on his face.

"Apparently." Adam ran his hand up her leg, stopping midway while her inner thighs tingled, aching for him to explore a bit further.

Ever since they'd arrived back at his house the day before, there had been nonstop visitors. Trudy began wondering if she would ever have a moment alone with the werewolf. Although if the ache growing deep inside her pussy was any indication, she needed hours and hours alone with Adam.

"Christopher Hordan's mother was a werewolf," Adam explained.

Margo sipped at her wine, her legs crossed as she looked up from where she sat on the floor next to John. Her soft brown eyes moved to watch Adam's hand stroke Trudy's leg, and she ran her tongue over her upper lip. Trudy felt a flush spread through her and took another sip of her wine. Maybe it was her imagination, but it looked like Margo started breathing faster while she watched Adam's fingers trace patterns along the inside of her leg. The ever so faint aroma of lust drifted through the air. This could prove to be an interesting night.

Trudy's breath caught in her throat, and she gripped Adam's shoulder just a bit harder than she meant to. He looked over at her, still talking, and then returned his attention to John. But Margo met her gaze, an unspoken reassurance appearing on her friend's face. Nothing would happen that she didn't want to happen.

But what if I want it to happen? Her heart skipped a beat when she remembered the night that John and Margo watched Adam fuck her. She took a deep breath, forcing herself to listen to what Adam was saying.

"According to what Mary told the authorities, her human grandfather raised them. I guess her grandmother's pack made life too difficult for her, and she gave up trying to maintain a den with a human."

"And Mary is Christopher Hordan's daughter?" Margo asked.

"Yes." Adam took a long gulp from the bottle of beer he had next to him, and then reclined further, pulling Trudy off the arm of the couch so that she cuddled next to him. "She was his only offspring who appeared to be all human. Hordan had enough werewolf in him that he could change, but not at will. It made living among humans very difficult for him."

"But he couldn't stay with his pack because he was too human," Margo guessed, standing up next to John and stretching.

Her large breasts outlined nicely through her shirt, full and round, her nipples puckering while her hands were above her head. Trudy glanced at Adam, knowing he had probably held them, maybe even sucked on them. Adam wasn't watching Margo though. He focused on the floor, or his hand maybe while he held Trudy's leg.

"What is going to happen to his family?" Trudy asked. "Mary has to face charges, I understand that. And her brother will be charged too, once he's out of the hospital. But what about Darla? What will happen to her?"

"It's up to Werewolf Affairs." Adam looked at her, those intense green eyes making her melt inside. Her heart picked up a beat while he studied her. "They lived with hatred all of their lives. All of them. It will take a lot of reeducation before any of them are released."

She nodded, understanding hatred and prejudice all too well. Her pack had shunned anyone who wasn't purebred *lunewulf*. She shook her head.

"I don't understand why we fear anyone who isn't just like us," she said.

She put her hand over Adam's. His large rugged hand, tanner than hers and speckled with black hair made her hand look like a child's. He took her hand in his, squeezing it.

"Not all werewolves are like that." John sounded defensive.

Trudy glanced up, his dark eyes, penetrating, causing a knot to form in her tummy. Excitement leaped through her. She licked her lips, her mouth suddenly dry. His scent seemed to grow strong while she studied him, rich and earthy, pure alpha.

"Would you?" Her voice cracked, and she cleared her throat, Margo turning to watch her. Heat flushed through Trudy but she held her own, her craving to fuck Adam having to be the reason why she suddenly felt so anxious. She focused her thoughts. "Would you take mixed breeds into your pack?"

"Sure." John shrugged. "Most American werewolves have mixed pedigrees."

"What if they were half-werewolf and half-human?" she challenged.

Margo glanced down at her mate, as if she wanted to hear his answer too.

John stroked his goatee, his expression serious while he watched her. "I never knew until this incident that we were compatible to breed with humans," he began, his words a slow drawl, drawn out like he considered each word before speaking. "But if approached, yes. I would take them in."

Margo smiled, squeezing her mate's shoulder.

Trudy believed him. She reached for her wineglass, taking a slow sip of the cool fluid and enjoying its tingling warmth when she swallowed.

Silence fell over the room, everyone contemplative over the events of the past few weeks. Trudy was all too aware of Adam's body pressed alongside hers on the couch though, his leg pressed against her outer leg, his hand holding hers. Her shoulder pressed against his biceps, the steel muscle reminding her of the strength and power he possessed.

There would always be prejudice and hatred. The world was full of it. Nothing she could do would wipe out those feelings in all werewolves. She would live among werewolves like her though, who cherished others for who they were, and not for their pedigree.

Taking another sip, she glanced up at Adam, admiring his strong profile, confidence and wisdom radiating from him even as he reclined on the sofa. He glanced down at her then lifted her hand to his mouth. She watched his white teeth scrape over her skin while those sultry green eyes devoured her.

The room suddenly seemed too warm, which had to be from the wine. She stood up, almost stumbling in her rush, and making everything spin around her for a brief moment.

"Does anyone else need something to drink?" she asked, deciding she would switch to ice water.

"I'll help you." Margo followed her to the kitchen after tapping John on the forehead when he held his almost empty beer bottle up.

Tingles rushed through Trudy, an excitement purging her system that she didn't understand. Electricity ran through the air, charged and raw, an anticipation that she couldn't shake.

She flipped the light switch on in Adam's kitchen, not sure of where everything was. Margo stood next to her, looking around at the modern appliances and glass-covered cabinets.

"Has he asked you to mate with him yet?" she asked.

Her question startled Trudy. "No." She moved to the counter, placing her hands on the cool hard surface. "He's been busy with Werewolf Affairs."

"I'm sure he will." Margo suddenly was behind her, her thin fingers massaging Trudy's shoulders.

She pressed deep into Trudy's muscles, her motions feeling good, easing a tension she didn't realize was there.

"I feel on edge," she confessed, staring down at her hands. "And I'm not sure why."

"You've been through a lot." Margo's scent wrapped around her, musky and alluring. "And now that it's over, you haven't had a chance to relax."

She hadn't had a chance to do anything. Her pussy throbbed, the flush she felt in the living room returning. Adam had been so busy debriefing over the phone as well as dealing with Bureau members arriving at his house, he'd barely had a minute for her. Now that the case was in Werewolf Affairs' hands, he needed to clear matters with John Campbell. Turning the evening into a social event had been Adam's idea, so that they could spend time together.

Trudy turned around, unable to handle Margo touching her any longer. The tingling in her shoulder muscles seemed to be sending rushes of heat straight through her body. She would fill the room with the smell of lust if she weren't careful.

She smiled, hoping her confidence showed. "Tonight is relaxing. Getting everything figured out with the werewolf killer, and knowing he is out of commission is a load off of my mind—and everyone's mind."

Margo nodded, her relaxed expression making Trudy wonder if the woman ever endured stress. She nodded toward the other room. "Those two will hash this out until they have themselves convinced they've saved the world."

Trudy almost laughed out loud.

"The way I understand the story, you saved Adam's ass." She lifted her finger, running it along Trudy's jaw line. Warmth from Margo's touch traveled through her, calming her, soothing her.

"More like his cock," she mumbled, and the two of them broke out in giggles.

In the next moment, Margo was kissing her. She didn't have time to react, to stop the action. What surprised her though, was that she was kissing Margo, too.

It was so different from kissing Adam. Not as real. Margo's lips were so soft, so warm, so tender. And her body, crushed against Trudy's wasn't hard like Adam's. Her full breasts pressed against Trudy's. The curve of her hip rubbed against Trudy's hipbone. And her touch, delicate and sensual, her long thin fingers brushing over Trudy's cheeks, drew her further into the kiss.

She didn't expect Margo to bite her. Well maybe it wasn't a bite, more like a nibble. She opened her eyes, along with her mouth, gasping in surprise. Margo's eyes were closed, her head slightly turned, a dark flush over her high cheekbones. She dug her fingers into Trudy's hair, pulling her mouth back to hers.

Their tongues met, swirling around each other's slowly. She tasted like wine, rich and aromatic. Trudy blinked her eyes closed, allowing Margo to tilt her head so she could deepen the kiss. The soft moan that rose up from her filled Trudy's mouth, feeding her, showing her how aroused Margo was.

Something inside Trudy stirred, a pressure building, a heat spreading through her that she hadn't expected. Did this turn her on? And if so, what should she do about it?

"Margo." John's baritone bounced off the walls.

Chapter Twenty-Five

"We discussed this." John gave Trudy a reprimanding look, while he slowly crossed his arms over his broad chest and stared at her.

"I know." Margo truly looked chastised. She took a step backward from Trudy.

"What did you discuss?" She frowned, looking from one of them to the other.

Adam moved in around John, and reached for her. A sensation brushed over her that she was being comforted, as if something had just happened that might have upset her.

"They think I'm trying to seduce you." Margo looked like she was pouting, her teeth pulling on her lower lip.

"Aren't you?" Suddenly she was confused. The three of them had discussed how Margo should behave when she was alone with Trudy. She had no idea when this conversation had transpired, but obviously Margo had been instructed how to act, or not act.

A small smile brushed over Margo's lips. "Well, I thought you wanted it, too."

Trudy opened her mouth to answer but then paused. What had she been just about to say? Looking from one of them to the other, she noticed encouragement on Margo. John's eyes looked darker than they had a second ago.

Looking up at Adam, her breath caught in her throat at the intensity of those green eyes. Everything around them seemed to fade. They were alone, just the two of them, their scents intertwining while heat from holding his hand surged through her, making his life force and hers one.

"I'm curious," she whispered, hardly able to utter the words.

Her heart began pounding furiously in her chest, the admission exciting and making her nervous all at once. The edge of his mouth twitched. A nerve, or the urge to smile, she didn't know. But those eyes captivated her, held on to her, pulled her into his strength, his intent desire to comfort her, see to her happiness.

"Okay." He didn't say anything more.

Heat rushed through her. Her pussy throbbed, so moist, so filled with an ache she couldn't appease. Searching his face, seeing his need also, an energy surged through her, strong and powerful, her bones popping before she realized her reaction to it.

Trudy sucked in a long, slow breath, never looking away from Adam. He seemed to feed her, his predatory nature so strong at the moment she could feel it wrapped around her like a warm blanket.

Suddenly she was moving, her feet not seeming to touch the ground. It was as if she floated, her body so light, so charged with energy that she tingled all over. Adam's arm wrapped around her, guiding her, holding her close. His heat surging through her, one with her own needs and lust.

Adam didn't bother to turn on the bedroom light when they entered. It didn't matter. Everything she needed was right within her grasp. Adam's strength, his power, his compassion, all of it saturated through her, feeding her. And looking up at him when he lowered her to the bed, she saw she fed him, too.

"What do you want, Trudy?" His voice was raw, hungry. He nipped at her neck while he asked.

"You." She didn't have to think to answer that question.

He chuckled, sending chills throughout her. She squirmed underneath him, his breath tickling her.

"You've already got me." He lifted himself above her, their faces mere inches from each other.

She already had him? Her thoughts were so muddled, emotions streaming through her so quickly. She couldn't think, couldn't focus on what he might mean by that.

"Do you want to play with Margo?" he asked her.

She suddenly felt foolish, realizing what he had meant with his question. "Will you watch?" she whispered.

Something dark appeared in his eyes, something carnal, his pupils altering their shape, just for a moment. The beast in him surfaced, his arousal too intense to keep it at bay.

"No one will ever touch you unless I am watching," he informed her, the seriousness in his tone stilling her heart.

Excitement flushed through her veins while blood pumped through her almost too fast for her human body. He had her pinned on the bed, his cock hard as steel pressed against her hip. She wanted to squirm, wrap herself around him, respond somehow with more than just words. His words marked her, the sensation of belonging to him, of him being her werewolf made her want to jump for joy.

"Good," was all she could think of to say, which seemed so lame in comparison to how his statement made her feel.

Exhilaration rushed through her when she sensed John and Margo in the doorway. Her pussy throbbed in anticipation, the pounding of her heart matching the beat in her cunt, moisture coating her, soaking her pants. The room filled with the smell of lust so quickly she knew it couldn't be all coming from her.

Margo moved forward, crawling on to the bed next to them. She spread out alongside Trudy, her fingers brushing over Adam's shoulder. Her eyes darted to the act, her insides tightening. She waited to feel jealousy, to experience a rage of protectiveness. She should be screaming, *hand's off. He's mine.*

But Adam never looked away from her, never changed his expression. He continued to pin her, to devour her with his predatory gaze. He paid no attention to Margo, and Margo didn't look at Adam. Her focus was on Trudy as well.

Her insides relaxed. This wasn't about a competition. No one wanted to take Adam from her. The knots in her stomach were replaced with a tight anticipation. She looked at Margo. Those gentle brown eyes glowed with lust. Her smooth black hair seemed a little bit out of place, as if John had ran his fingers through it, messed it up a bit. Her full dark red lips glistened with moisture. She leaned forward, pressing against both of them.

"I am going to enjoy you," she whispered.

Trudy thought she would come just from that promise. The ache in her pussy demanded attention and she struggled under Adam, desperate to ease the growing pain.

It looked like Adam endured some pain of his own when he moved off of her. "I'm not sure how long I can wait for my turn," he warned.

He wanted her. That knowledge filled her with more desire and yearning than she thought she could handle.

"She wants you too," Margo said, her voice a husky whisper. "Just look at her."

"I am looking at her." Adam slid off the bed, revealing the hard shaft that pressed against his pants.

Trudy sucked in her breath, finally able to reach for the spot that ached the most. Her own moisture had soaked through her pants, the material damp and hot when she put her fingers on the spot that needed attention most. Pressure shifted inside her when she rubbed herself, the ache growing, anticipation filling her, while lust filled the air so thickly around her she thought she would be drunk off of it.

"Look at them watching you." Margo's breath was hot against her cheek, her friend's hands already stroking her skin under her shirt. "They are adoring your beauty, Trudy. Look at them."

She glanced up past Margo, who was intent on removing Trudy's shirt, and saw the two werewolves hovering over them. Their eyes glowed, their expressions serious. Concentration on keeping their own needs at bay kept them still.

Margo pulled Trudy's shirt over her head and at the same time she felt fingers fumbling on her jeans buttons.

"It amazes me how you are more beautiful every time I see you." Adam pressed his lips to her skin, kissing her just inside her hipbone while he pulled her jeans down.

Fire seared through her skin where his mouth touched her. Rushes of passion rippled through her, exploding inside her. She would have cried out, her orgasm stronger than she expected, but Margo covered her mouth, stealing her breath, her kiss hot and aggressive.

Trudy seized the action, her tongue dancing with Margo's while she wrapped her arms around the woman, surprised to feel she was naked. She didn't remember her clothes coming off, and in her fogged senses thought John must have had a play in that.

"My hot little bitch is absolutely soaked." Adam's mouth hovered over her pussy, his fingers pressing against her skin, stroking around her most sensitive spots.

"She isn't the only one." John's voice sounded gravelly.

Margo groaned into Trudy's mouth, raking her fingernails over the sensitive skin of Trudy's breast, teasing her nipple. Trudy arched into her touch, crying out into their kiss as her tender nipple was teased. She thought she would come again, worried they would take everything she had to offer and still want more from her. But the throbbing pulse in her pussy didn't seem to subside. Adam's breath tortured her, he seemed to be running his fingers over every inch of her, making her want to grab his head, and force him between her legs.

"Trudy." Margo broke off their kiss. "Your energy. Your passion. All of your scents are so wonderful."

Trudy swore she had been drowning and was just let up for air. She gasped, struggling to catch her breath.

Adam's tongue darted across her pussy, dipping in between the folds and lapping at her heat. She cried out, arching into him, needing him to suck more, lick more, appease the ache that was about to make her crazy.

"This is too much." Yet she wanted more. Craved more. Never wanted this to end.

Adam chuckled, moist heat causing her pussy to burn. If he didn't fuck her soon she knew she wouldn't make it. She would end up begging, crying, doing anything for him to relieve the deep throbbing pain that swelled inside her cunt.

"May I taste her too? Please?" Margo had already slid around Trudy, the thick sensual aroma of her sex surrounding Trudy.

"Come down here." John moved to position his mate, draw her to the end of the bed.

Trudy watched him grip Margo's ass, his large hands pressing into her smooth caramel-colored skin. The action had her wiggling, caressing the pearl-hard nub between her legs that craved satisfaction.

Adam slipped up next to her, his green eyes glowing, intense passion burning through his gaze, searing her skin wherever he looked.

Margo covered Trudy's pussy with her mouth. Trudy jumped, distracted by Adam's possessive stare. He gripped her chin, ignoring what Margo was doing to her, and moved so that his face was mere inches from hers.

"So beautiful," he whispered, before devouring her mouth.

His teeth had grown just enough to prick the corner of her lip when he pressed his lips to hers. But the sweet pain only added to the intensity of the kiss.

Margo gently spread her sensitive folds, her tongue soft and soothing, yet at the same time building the fire that spread through her so rapidly she could hardly breathe.

Adam's fingers on her chin, on her neck, holding her head in place, while his tongue probed deep inside her mouth, put her over the edge. She swirled her tongue around his, growing drunk on his passion. Gripping his shoulders, digging her fingers into the strength of his body, she soared higher than she ever had before.

"That's it, baby," Margo purred.

Trudy felt Margo's face pushed harder into her pussy, and broke away from Adam's kiss, looking down at her queen bitch. John had entered his mate from behind. Margo stared up at her, her mouth forming an adorable circle while her eyes glazed over.

"Oh. John." Margo barely uttered the words, while he fucked her hard from behind.

In all of her sexual experiences, she'd never seen another woman fucked. Watching in awe, she realized she had reached down for Adam's cock, and wondered when he'd managed to get out of his clothes.

She gripped his huge, rock-hard shaft, stroking it, pulling it toward her, while she watched in awe the spectacular scene playing out in front of her. Margo rested her cheek on Trudy's pussy, her skin flushed. She trapped the heat between Trudy's legs, while John stood behind her.

Trudy studied his naked chest, sprinkled with black curly hair, with corded muscles rippling under his dark skin. She found herself comparing him to Adam. John was handsome, damned sexy. He was large and dominating, the way she would expect a pack leader to be. But he didn't hold a flame to Adam.

"That's it, baby." Margo lifted her cheek off of Trudy's skin, leaving it soaked, sweltering, the ache building beyond her control. "Fuck me, damnit. Fuck me hard."

John increased his speed. He pounded his mate, the smell of their sex soaking the room, rich and intoxicating. Trudy watched while his facial muscles contorted, his jaw widening while his teeth grew. She almost exploded when he threw back his head, howling while he released himself into his mate.

"Yes." Margo arched her back, her expression pure bliss. "Oh hell yes."

She smiled at Trudy then collapsed on top of her, the fire from her body almost burning Trudy's skin.

Trudy turned her attention back to Adam, surprised to see him watching her. "I need you," she whispered, unable to put into words that she would die if he didn't fuck her soon.

"Oh. You will have me. And soon." His smile made her heart stop, her mouth suddenly dry while she stared into raw lust.

Chapter Twenty-Six

Trudy stood naked in the living room, focusing on John and Margo's footsteps after Adam closed the door. Her body screamed so loudly for release she needed to give her attention to the small things, anything, just to maintain sanity.

Her pussy pulsed, throbbed, cum soaking her every time she moved. Listening to their shoes crunch against the gravel while they walked to their car, she did her best to keep herself focused.

Adam shut the door, tapping the buttons on his security panel on the wall, and then turned. She didn't have to look up to know he devoured her with green eyes she could drown in.

"I've never met anyone like you." His voice was husky, gravelly, the beast within him speaking through his human mouth.

She hoped his comment was a good one. From the smell of him she knew it was, but hesitation still struggled through her, fighting with the lust that ransacked her body.

"Nor I you." She dared to look up at him, meet his gaze. Power and domination seemed to glow around him, the scent was so thick.

Roped muscles twitched under his skin, making her itch to run her fingers along his chest, play with the scattered curls of hair.

His entire body was hard, all male, a perfect specimen, the definition of Alpha male in his prime. No one would ever conquer him, he would always be the watcher of packs, peacekeeper for all werewolves. The huge responsibility seemed to fit perfectly on his shoulders, as if his breeding would allow him no smaller role.

She tingled all over just staring at him, emotions running so rampant through her system they took her breath away. He moved toward her and she thought her heart might explode. Her mouth went dry, then seemed to wet, while she watched him until he stood within mere inches of her, their bodies almost touching.

"I want you with me." He looked down at her, not touching her, even though she could feel him everywhere. He searched her face, looking for a reaction to his words. "Trudy. Tell me you will stay by my side, hunt with me, run with me under the moon."

"Yes." Her voice wouldn't work. The one word escaped her lips a mere whisper.

"I want to feed you my kill." Still he didn't touch her, his body motionless, power radiating from him and scouring through her.

Her legs seemed weak from the intensity of strength that soaked through her, standing within inches of him.

"Yes," she said, this time more audible.

"Every morning I will wake with you by my side. And at night, you will be the last sight I enjoy before falling asleep."

She had never known he could be so romantic. Emotions surged through her so fiercely she thought she might make a fool out of herself and start crying.

She took a deep breath. "I want that too."

He moved his hand, the action seeming to play out in slow motion. Large powerful fingers, the strength in them alone enough to kill. But when he touched her skin, stroked her cheek, she thought she would melt from his gentleness.

"You are my mate." He whispered these words, the sacredness of them rushing through her, turning her insides into molten lava.

"And you are my mate." She couldn't stand it any longer. Leaning into him, pressing against the iron muscles burning with heat, she wrapped her arms around his neck, allowing herself to drown in those devastatingly handsome green eyes. "I love you, Adam Knight."

A small smile tugged at his lips. "I want to hear that a hundred more times." He brushed his lips over hers. "And I love you."

The breath from his words fed her soul, making her somehow stronger, an even match for the deadly werewolf she clung to.

He lifted her with such little effort he made her feel light as a feather. And she knew she wasn't that small of a woman. His body seemed to move as one while he carried her through the living room, and back to his bedroom. She could still see the indentions in the blankets from where she had laid while Margo enjoyed her, and while she watched John fuck Margo.

"Did you enjoy your experience?" Adam seemed to sense her thoughts.

"Yes." And she had. "But all I really want is you."

She wasn't sure but it seemed his chest swelled a bit, his all male scent growing stronger, pride sneaking its way through. He didn't let go when he lowered her onto the bed, consuming her view with his powerful body.

"Well it's my duty to please my mate," he drawled, lightening the mood a bit as if aware of the emotions she detected and wanting her to see him as a werewolf confident enough to handle all situations.

Wrapping her legs around him, she reached between them, taking hold of the powerful shaft ready to impale her.

"I'm going to need a lot of pleasing." She smiled up at him, enjoying the growl that rumbled through him.

She almost couldn't get her hands out of the way fast enough before he rammed deep inside her, filling her with his cock, electricity racing through her with a violent shudder.

"Oh God." She screamed, knowing he would fuck her, but not ready for the intensity of his penetration.

Adam moved to his knees, taking a hold of her legs, spreading her, adjusting the angle. His cock glided out of her only to dive deep inside her again. Bright lights clouded her vision as if she had just had the wind knocked out of her. But never had she enjoyed such a blow as the one he'd given her. His movements were quick, solid, never hesitating. He slammed into her cunt again and again, filling her, releasing the dam that had held back the many orgasms aching to flow through her.

She screamed, arching into him, wanting all he could give her. Never had he felt so good inside her. No one had ever brought her such fulfillment. And still he didn't subside.

It took some effort to focus, but she ached to see his face, to watch the incredible Alpha male claiming her, giving her the honor she never dreamed she would possess. His expression was determined, his jaw set, his hooded gaze filled with lust and love while muscles rippled through him with every thrust.

More pressure built inside her, yet another orgasm threatening to escape within her pussy. She didn't know she could come so much. Watching Adam watch her, she did her best to reach out, to touch the solid chest beaming with sweat before her.

Mine. Every bit of him is mine!

She wanted to shout the words, to announce to the world, to every pack, to every female on the planet that she had mated with the best of Alphas. Her life was full now, her soul mate intact. Pleasure rippled through her, love billowing through her like a strong gust of wind.

"I love you," she cried out, just as she came again, drowning when he exploded inside her.

The heat between them was almost unbearable, but at the same time soothing when he lowered himself over her.

"And I love you, Trudy Knight."

She loved the sound of her new name, whispered from the lips of the werewolf she knew had always been destined to be hers. Wrapping her arms around him, she rested comfortably on top of him when he rolled over, keeping her close.

All was safe with the world, and with her. Slowly, she drifted off to sleep.

Dear Lord. Miss Beth Parks had filled out nicely. He blew out a breath of air, realizing he would start drooling if he didn't take his mind off of that small but perfectly shaped body. She would look damned good sprawled out on a bed. He'd begun to wonder whether she shaved her pussy or not when he gave himself a mental slap.

"Contact City Hall," she was saying. "I don't want to go in front of the judge in a court room. It's best to keep a low profile here. Let him know I'll meet with him in his chambers and we'll keep this short and sweet."

Ethan realized at that moment that Sandra Parks sat at the kitchen table, watching him carefully. Greta Hothmeyer sat across from her, also watching him, satisfaction filling the air from the two of them.

This had gone far enough. Intercepting Beth in mid-pace, he put his hand over her phone. She looked up at him, possibly noticing him for the first time, or maybe realizing for the first time who he was. Something akin to panic rushed through her, the strong confidence that had swarmed around her a moment before gone. It lasted only a moment before the spicy smell of irritation floated in the air between them. And there wasn't much space between them.

"Hang up that phone before I hang it up for you," he whispered, enjoying the worried expression his implied threat caused.

"You do not tell me what to do." She matched his threatening tone quite well.

Amusement rushed through him, his loins tightening with the reminder of what a spitfire she was. It made sense if she was some hotshot lawyer. But she wasn't so good that he couldn't take her on. Maybe when they were cubs she'd managed to get the better of him, making a fool of him in front of all of their peers. But that had been a long time ago. He was in charge here. No matter how many people she might be used to bossing around, this saucy little bitch would learn here and now, she would do as he told her.

Squeezing down on her hand just enough to make his point, he removed her phone, and pushed the off button. A look of disbelief crossed her face.

"How dare you!" She put her hands on her hips, her lips pursing in anger. Her dark green eyes sparked with fire, but it was the tell-tale flush that spread across her cheeks that gave him the urge to press her up against the counter and show her exactly what he would dare to do.

He could have it out with her right here in the kitchen, but he needed some time. This wasn't one of the sweet little bitches he was accustomed to who drooled every time he walked into the room. Beth Parks didn't appear the least bit intimidated by him, even though she barely stood tall enough to reach his shoulders. The fire in her expression let him see her passion. She lusted over him. He knew it. But she had it well hidden. Just like she had so many years ago when they were cubs.

There was only one thing to do.

Ethan grabbed Beth by the arm and turned to walk out of the house.

"What the hell are you doing?" Beth sounded alarmed, although if she was trying to stop him, she wasn't very strong. It seemed she followed him through the house willingly.

"What's going on?" Ralph asked.

Ethan ignored the group and stormed to the front door, dragging Beth behind him.

"I'll call you in a bit," Ethan told him, knowing Ralph would be able to calm the group.

Ethan needed time to sort things out, and to think with his brain and not his cock.

The smells of the house faded quickly when they marched across the front yard. He knew every pack member watched them but he didn't care. He almost threw Beth at his bike.

"If you think I'm going to get on that thing..." she began.

He grabbed her shoulders, fighting the urge to press himself against her, just for a moment, wanting to see how she felt up against him. Instead he simply looked her square in the eye, all too aware of the heat that surged through his hands where he touched her.

"You can climb on, or I will throw you on." He enjoyed how her eyes grew wide, the all-knowing counselor suddenly at a loss for words. "But either way, we are going for a ride."

"How in the hell did you manage to become pack leader?" she mumbled, anger seeping from her. The spicy scent of it lay cover to something more evocative, more sultry. A scent he hadn't noticed while they were in the kitchen grabbed his attention now.

Beth Parks was more than aroused. She had to be soaking wet. What he wouldn't do to run his hand down between the crotch of her jeans, feel her heat.

Since she hadn't moved, he decided she must want to be lifted on to his bike. It was a large Harley, and she was a petite woman. Grabbing her by the waist, he lifted her high enough for her to straddle the small passenger seat.

"How dare you!" Beth squirmed in his arms, her legs going everywhere but around his bike.

Ethan heard definite laughter coming from the house. Well the last thing the counselor would do was make a fool out of him—again. Placing her back down on the ground, before she kicked something that might really put him out of commission, he twisted her around, bent her over his bike, and gave her rear end a quick swat.

"Shit!" she cried out loud enough to make everyone in the neighborhood aware of their presence.

Beth turned on him with her fist raised, ready to do damage. Her dark green eyes glowed with anger, those soft lips barely covering teeth that had started to sharpen.

Ethan grabbed her fist, pulling her to him. He could feel her heart pounding between her breasts. And those full round mounds pressed against him felt better than anything he'd experienced in quite a while. He held on to her hand, while pinning her other arm between them. His free hand strolled down her back. And it took some effort not to cup that sweet ass of hers.

"Now," he said quietly. "You may climb on, or I will lift you on. But you are getting on that bike. I will not have a yelling match with you in the middle of this neighborhood."

Beth considered his words, her heavy breathing causing her breasts to move against his chest. She struggled to free herself and he tightened his grip.

"What's it going to be, counselor?" he asked.

"I will not be bullied." Even captured in his arms she would fight him. "Let go of me now, unless you wish to spend the night in jail."

Ethan smiled. Her idle threats didn't bother him a bit. There was no way anyone would arrest him for taking on the mouthy lawyer. They might want to watch. His grin widened.

"Are you accustomed to people backing down simply because you threaten them?"

"I'm accustomed to dealing with werewolves who have manners." She fought again to be released.

"I can be very polite." He pulled her just a bit closer, her breath scorching through his chest, burning his skin. "I don't know why you bring out the beast in me," he whispered, lowering his head so that her face was inches from his.

About the author:

All my life, I've wondered at how people fall into the routines of life. The paths we travel seemed to be well-trodden by society. We go to school, fall in love, find a line of work (and hope and pray it is one we like), have children and do our best to mold them into good people who will travel the same path. This is the path so commonly referred to as the "real world".

The characters in my books are destined to stray down a different path other than the one society suggests. Each story leads the reader into a world altered slightly from the one they know. For me, this is what good fiction is about, an opportunity to escape from the daily grind and wander down someone else's path.

Lorie O'Clare lives in Kansas with her three sons.

Lorie welcomes mail from readers. You can write to her c/o Ellora's Cave Publishing at 1337 Commerce Drive, Suite 13, Stow OH 44224.

Why an electronic book?

We live in the Information Age—an exciting time in the history of human civilization in which technology rules supreme and continues to progress in leaps and bounds every minute of every hour of every day. For a multitude of reasons, more and more avid literary fans are opting to purchase e-books instead of paperbacks. The question to those not yet initiated to the world of electronic reading is simply: *why?*

1. *Price.* An electronic title at Ellora's Cave Publishing runs anywhere from 40-75% less than the cover price of the <u>exact same title</u> in paperback format. Why? Cold mathematics. It is less expensive to publish an e-book than it is to publish a paperback, so the savings are passed along to the consumer.

2. *Space.* Running out of room to house your paperback books? That is one worry you will never have with electronic novels. For a low one-time cost, you can purchase a handheld computer designed specifically for e-reading purposes. Many e-readers are larger than the average handheld, giving you plenty of screen room. Better yet, hundreds of titles can be stored within your new library—a single microchip. (Please note that Ellora's Cave does not endorse any specific brands. You can check our website at www.ellorascave.com for customer recommendations we make available to new consumers.)

3. *Mobility.* Because your new library now consists of only a microchip, your entire cache of books can be taken with you wherever you go.

4. *Personal preferences are accounted for.* Are the words you are currently reading too small? Too large? Too...**ANNOYING**? Paperback books cannot be modified according to personal preferences, but e-books can.

5. *Innovation.* The way you read a book is not the only advancement the Information Age has gifted the literary community with. There is also the factor of what you can read. Ellora's Cave Publishing will be introducing a new line of interactive titles that are available in e-book format only.

6. *Instant gratification.* Is it the middle of the night and all the bookstores are closed? Are you tired of waiting days—sometimes weeks—for online and offline bookstores to ship the novels you bought? Ellora's Cave Publishing sells instantaneous downloads 24 hours a day, 7 days a week, 365 days a year. Our e-book delivery system is 100% automated, meaning your order is filled as soon as you pay for it.

Those are a few of the top reasons why electronic novels are displacing paperbacks for many an avid reader. As always, Ellora's Cave Publishing welcomes your questions and comments. We invite you to email us at service@ellorascave.com or write to us directly at: 1337 Commerce Drive, Suite 13, Stow OH 44224.

Discover for yourself why readers can't get enough of the multiple award-winning publisher Ellora's Cave. Whether you prefer e-books or paperbacks, be sure to visit EC on the web at www.ellorascave.com for an erotic reading experience that will leave you breathless.

WWW.ELLORASCAVE.COM

Printed in the United States
29403LVS00003B/187-237